WHITE INDIAN BOY
Duane R. Lund

based on the adventures of john tanner
THE LAKE OF THE WOODS FALCON

Printed in U.S.A.

ISBN 0-934860-17-3

Table of Contents

FOREWORD

Few men become a legend in their own time, but John Tanner was such a man.

Born in 1780 in Virginia. . .the son of missionary parents. . .kidnapped from the Kentucky shores of the Ohio River at age 10 by the Shawnee . . .sold to an Ottawa family who loved him as their own son . . .it was his privilege to be raised among the Algonquin Indian tribes at a time when they still lived much as they had for generations before the coming of the white man.

In later years, Tanner became leader of his own band of Indians on the Lake of the Woods. In that capacity he—

- defended his people against exploitation by certain traders,
- served as a soldier of fortune to Lord Selkirk of the Hudson's Bay Company, leading his own braves and a group of fifty Swiss mercenaries in the recapture of a string of forts which had been taken over by the rival Northwest Company,
- helped Dr. Edwin James, an army surgeon, translate the New Testament into Ojibway,
- and guided the famous explorer and Indian Agent Henry Schoolcraft.

Although this book describes historic places and people of the late 1700's and early 1800's, it is not intended to be a history. And, although it is based on Tanner's own narrative as told to Dr. Edwin James at Sault Ste. Marie in 1830, it is not a biography. An honest effort has been made to remain faithful to the Tanner narrative, but some of the events are reported out of sequence and, of course, much is left out. There are also embellishments to provide greater opportunity for descriptions of the Indian's culture and way of life—how he hunted, fished, trapped, fought, endured hardships, enjoyed nature and supported his family.

So read on and enjoy the story of Johnny Tanner, the white Indian boy, from age ten through his "teens", as he lives out the dream of many a youth who has longed to grow up as an Indian back in the days when this great people ruled the vast wilderness of North America.

CHAPTER I
KIDNAPPED!

Johnny knew better.

His father had given him strict orders to stay in the house. Indians had been seen in the area and it was rumored they were out for revenge. A few weeks earlier several young braves—drunk with rum—had terrified the settlement up river. Before the disturbance was over two of them had been killed by the frightened whites.

But the first genuine warm spring afternoon made the out-of-doors seem so attractive. Through the kitchen window Johnny could see the buds on the trees—so big they looked like they could burst into leaves any minute. There wasn't a cloud in the sky and the Ohio River reflected pure blue as it wound its way past the Tanner homestead. How he envied his brother, Edward, as he worked in the field with their father, the Reverend John Tanner, Sr., planting corn. Occasionally, the strong voice of the "minister-farmer", carried on the warm May breezes, drifted through the open door from across the fields. Johnny wanted to be out there, too. The whole world was coming to life and he was stuck in the house—"cooped up," he thought to himself, "like being in a cage."

The temptation was almost more than any normal, healthy, ten-year-old boy could bear.

From upstairs came the cry of his baby brother—telling the whole world he was awake and demanding to be fed. Mrs. Tanner summoned Johnny's two younger sisters from the next room and ordered them upstairs to comfort the child. The crying continued. In his misery, Johnny was scarcely aware of the noise. Mrs. Tanner heard it all right, but she tried to ignore the baby while she peeled the last few potatoes she was preparing for the evening meal. The cries grew louder and sadder, and her motherly instincts finally prevailed. In exasperation she laid aside the paring knife. As Mrs. Tanner arose from the kitchen table she turned to Johnny and spoke sternly, "Now stay put, young man. I'm going upstairs to tend to your brother and make the beds. You know what your father said about staying in the house. If you get your school work done, there will be plenty of daylight after supper for your pa to take you down to the river. So get at your studies instead of sitting there day-dreaming."

Johnny looked up at his mother and sighed, but made no move towards his books.

"Johnny, do you hear me!?" Mrs. Tanner asked as severely as she could without sounding unkind. She could not forget that she was the older boys' stepmother and never felt quite comfortable being cross with them.

"Yes, ma," the boy muttered in exasperation, making it clear he didn't appreciate being treated like a prisoner in his own home or being told to study on a day meant for living.

As the sound of his mother's footsteps faded up the stairs, temptation overwhelmed him. Johnny knew it would be a good half-hour before she returned—plenty of time to run down to the river and back. Maybe he could catch a glimpse of fish spawning in the creek or sneak up on the hen mallard that had made her nest in the tall grass on the bank.

After tiptoeing out the door, Johnny ran as fast as his legs could carry him across the yard and down the hill. As he neared the place where the creek poured into the Ohio River, he slowed to a walk, and then carefully parted the hazel brush for a good view of the stream—nothing. He should have known the fish wouldn't run at midday—or were they done spawning? Well, he'd just check on that old hen mallard and give her a real scare! He crawled on his hands through last year's dead grass to the spot. Carefully he poked his face through the dried-up cattail stalks where he and his brother had accidentally flushed the quacking mallard from her nest a few days earlier. But, nothing. She was off feeding and the boy had to look ever so closely to count the eleven eggs which had been so craftily hidden under the dry grass and duck down.

What to do? He'd spy on his father and brother! He knew if his father saw him he'd be in for a good licking and probably be sent to bed without a bite to eat. Silently but swiftly he ran along the shore, using the high river bank for cover. Upon reaching the corner of the field, he crawled up the steep incline on his hands and knees. As he reached the top he found little vegatation to conceal himself, but thought he could reach a fairly thick clump of bushes by wiggling through the weeds on his stomach. No problem! He was there in seconds. By raising himself on his elbows he could see his father and brother on "all fours" at the far end of the field making little hills of earth with their hands and planting three kernels of corn in each one. Johnny became aware of some objects, round and hard, under his body—walnuts!—and he began to gather them.

Then it happened! There was no warning—not even the crunch of dead grass or the snap of a twig. A big hand was slapped so tightly over his mouth and nose that he couldn't breathe! Other hands squeezed the muscles in his arms so violently he feared his bones would break. In a flash his feet were off the ground. Johnny felt like he was flying through the air with a big Indian warrior on either side! In seconds they were at the river where a third brave held a canoe in knee-deep water. Only then did his captors let him catch his breath. But the big hand remained firmly over Johnny's mouth. The second Indian, releasing his grasp on the boy's arm, stepped into the water and gracefully climbed into the canoe, settling in the bow on his knees. Without removing the hand from Johnny's face, the other brave placed a muscular arm across the boy's chest, pulled him tightly against his body, and with one swoop lifted his captive into the canoe and then stepped in himself and sat down behind him—still holding the trembling body like a vice. Quickly the third warrior, who had been guarding the canoe, pushed the craft out into the stream, crawled into the stern—and they were off, their silent paddles never breaking water. The Indians guided the canoe along the shore where the high bank hid them from view of the Tanner homestead and fields.

Everything had happened too quickly for Johnny to think or take any action on his own. But as his mind cleared he realized the farther he was carried from his home the less was his chance of escape or rescue. He decided his only hope was to immediately overturn or capsize the canoe. With all his might he struck the heel of his boot against the bottom of the hickory bark boat and at the same time tried to wrench free. The warrior's muscular arm only squeezed tighter, but the blow from his boot opened a seam and water squirted in like a little fountain. He raised his leg to strike again but this time the Indian was ready. A big forearm came up under the boy's knees and cradled him against the brave's chest so tightly that once again he could scarcely breathe. The man in the bow turned upon hearing the commotion, pulled a tomahawk from his waistband and shook it menacingly under Johnny's nose. He got the point and resigned himself to his fate—at least for the time being—and let his body go limp in the grasp of his captor.

When well out in the river and beyond voice range, the brave who held him took his hand away from Johnny's face but did not relax the hold on his body. Slowly, Johnny turned his head and nervously looked up at his captor. To his amazement, the big Indian was smiling. But it wasn't a friendly smile. It was more a smile of satisfaction. . .a smile of victory. . .a smile that said, "We pulled it off—we've gotcha!"

The break Johnny had opened in the bottom of the fragile canoe was not big—but water continued to gurgle through the seam and the accumulation forced the big Indian to raise up on his haunches. When a sandbar appeared ahead in mid-stream, the man who held him softly spoke an order and the paddlers turned the craft to dry land. While the big Indian held the boy draped over his arm the others turned the canoe upside down. Spruce gum appeared from nowhere and was jammed into the crack. Within seconds the vessel was uprighted and slid into the water. The warrior with the tomahawk once again seized his weapon, pointed at the mended crack and alternately shook the ax under Johnny's nose and pointed it at the sky, all of which the boy took to mean, "There'd better not be any more monkey business or you might as well prepare to meet your maker!"

Johnny vigorously nodded his head, showing that he understood and agreed. The brave scowled once more for good measure and then picked up his paddle and went back to work.

As the canoe continued to charge cross stream, propelled by the husky paddlers and pushed by the swollen waters of the big Ohio, Johnny began to study his captors. He decided there was good reason the man who held him was larger than the other two. He was older, and they were so young, probably in their teens, surely not much older than his own brother, Edward. "I've been kidnapped by a father and his sons," he surmised to himself.

Johnny was right.

All three were dressed only in loin cloths and moccasins, revealing well-muscled bodies that made Johnny feel terribly puny and weak when he looked at his own spindly arms. For the first time it occurred to him that the braves did not wear warpaint—but that was small consolation in view of the circumstances in which he found himself. But the fact that he was still alive and that he hadn't been scalped gave him hope.

Clouds now appeared and the sky, once so bright and so blue, began to darken and Johnny's thoughts darkened with it.

"Maybe they are bringing me back to torture me for the entertainment of the tribe!"

"Maybe I'll be burned at a stake or slowly roasted by a fire while the tribe enjoys revenge for the death of those two Indians at the settlement."

"Maybe I'm going to be a white slave; maybe the Indians have gotten some ideas from watching the black slaves working in the fields along the river."

"Maybe the Indians will take me so far away I'll never see home again."

At the thought of home, Johnny's thoughts grew still darker:

". . .wonder what Ma thought when she came downstairs. . ."

"She probably went screaming out to the fields. . ."

"I'll bet Pa was really mad."

"I wonder if anybody cried when they found I was gone?"

"Maybe even Ed cried. . .naw."

"They're probably having supper now, and my chair's empty."

The vision of the empty chair did it. Johnny began to cry. First there was a whimper or two, then came the tears. And as his tortured mind filled with thoughts of the warm kitchen and a fire leaping in the hearth, the boy broke into uncontrollable sobbing. Slowly the big Indian relaxed his hold and motioned for Johnny to sit on the floor of the canoe. Impressed by this first indication that his captors might be human after all, he managed to control his sobbing and wiped his eyes with the sleeve of his shirt.

At this point they entered the mouth of the Big Miami River (which entered the Ohio on the opposite shore from the Tanner homestead). The big Indian grunted a word as he pointed towards the far bank. Johnny was able to make out a canoe paddle that had been planted in the weeds and mud as a marker. Minutes later, the young brave in the bow stepped into nearly waist-deep water and steadied the canoe while the others disembarked. The vessel was hidden in the woods and one of the boys ran down the shore, returning a minute or two later with three blankets, a kettle and a pouch.

The Indians apparently felt they had the jump on any rescue party and sat down to catch their breath. Johnny chose to move around and stretch his cramped muscles and he was soon prancing around the tall grass like a young fawn. Suddenly a wild turkey, which had been crouching in terror over her nest ever since the party landed, exploded into the air. Johnny forgot his predicament for the moment and ran to the spot where the bird had taken flight. Sure enough—there were six huge eggs. Then recalling where he was, he scooped them up and brought them to the lead Indian as sort of a peace offering. The gesture brought the right response. The Indians exchanged glances and then broke into laughter. Even Johnny laughed, but a bit nervously.

A fire was kindled and the eggs placed in a pot of water to boil. But the meal was to be postponed. Around the point at the mouth of the river, first one canoe and then another and another came into view. Trees and rushes along the bank pretty well hid the Indians and their captives for the moment, and the fire was quickly doused with water from the kettle. One of the younger braves put the turkey eggs back in the empty kettle as the others quickly gathered their few belongings and took to the woods. The older Indian located a path he apparently knew was there and the four hurried on at a trot. The men ran in the same order in which they had sat in the canoe, and the Indian father pushed Johnny ahead of him with the fingers of his big hand entwined in the boy's shirt collar.

The ordeals of the day soon began to take their effect on the ten-year-old and he stumbled again and again on the trail, but the firm hand of the big man never let him fall. As evening came and the trail darkened, Johnny wondered how his captors could find their way. At long last, the leader called a halt and pointed to some fairly level ground that was somewhat softened by a carpet of wintergreen plants. Smoked fish was extracted from the mysterious pouch that had been retrieved from hiding shortly after the canoe had landed. Up until now Johnny had given no thought to food, but the smell of the smoked meat suddenly made him very hungry. With drooling mouth he watched the three eat their fill; some of the leftovers were finally offered to him. Johnny devoured them so fast he even swallowed a few bones. Fortunately none stuck in his throat.

Apparently satisfied they had not been followed, the men lay down to sleep. Johnny was pulled to the ground between the father and the older of the two sons; they lay so close together that a single blanket covered all three of them. Johnny stayed awake, hoping for a chance to escape. He tried to fill his mind with thoughts of what he would do if he once got out of their sight. He thought too about the boats they had seen. Could they have been carrying his father and Edward and some of the neighbors from the settlement? But his body was bone-aching tired and Johnny was the first to fall asleep.

That night, Johnny Tanner dreamed the first of hundreds of dreams he would have about his home and his family—a family he would not see again until he was a man!

CHAPTER II
ADOPTED

When Johnny awoke, he was surprised to find that both of his "bed partners" were already up and stirring about in the soft light of dawn. Before he could get to his feet, the older Indian, who Johnny had decided was the father of the two younger braves, squatted down and quickly unlaced the boy's boots and slipped them off, tossing them as far as he could into the woods. The sudden move upset Johnny and puzzled him. He never did figure out whether the intent was to help him run faster or to keep him from leaving telltale shoe prints in the path as clues for any would-be rescuers who might follow. The sleepy-eyed boy had little time to consider the issue as a calloused hand grabbed his arm and jerked him to his feet. Then they were off at a trot—through the forest, along the edges of muddy swamps, across waist-deep creeks, up steep hillsides, over fallen trees—and on and on.

Johnny tried to take notice of each landmark so that he could find his way back should he escape. Not forgetting the possibility of being rescued, he tried, when not watched, to leave signs for followers—a footprint deep in the mud, a broken branch, a scrape mark in the middle of the path. With his mind so completely occupied with thoughts of escape or rescue, Johnny scarcely noticed his sore feet or empty stomach. But hope turned to despair before the day was over, on two accounts: first, just as the four were scrambling down a brushy hillside, a war party of a score or more of painted warriors appeared in the valley below. Johnny's captors quickly exchanged glances, then a smile of recognition crossed the big man's face and he spoke a word of assurance to sons, "Shawnee". Johnny did not know it, but his captors were also of that tribe.

They hurried forward to meet the oncoming braves. After considerable talk the war party went on its way in the direction from which the kidnappers had come. The younger of the Indian boys touched Johnny's shoulder to get his attention. He then took his tomahawk from his waistband, pointed after the departing war party, and then sank the hatchet into an imaginary skull—three times for emphasis. As Johnny looked up at the teenager and saw the half smile-half sneer on his face, he knew only too well that the war party intended to intercept any rescue group that may have followed. Weeks later, when Johnny had learned enough Shawnee to communicate fairly well, he was told that the Indians did indeed intercept a rescue mission and several men were killed or wounded on both sides. It was not known to either Johnny or his captors, but having been turned back by the war party, the whites had decided to give up their search for the time being.

And then, another disappointment. As they reached the bottom of the valley a swift and apparently deep stream brought them to a momentary halt. With a swoop, the father lifted Johnny to his shoulders and waded in. The water swirled and gurgled around the big man's chest as he reached the deepest part. The boy knew escape would now be useless; there was no way he could cross that river alone even if he should get away. Not only was the water too deep but the current was too strong to swim. As the brave's huge hands lifted Johnny off his shoulders and set his feet once again on dry ground, the ten year old looked back with an audible sigh, a sigh that was almost a whimper. He knew he had just passed the point of no return.

With only an occasional stop to eat smoked fish from the pouch they carried or to sip a drink from a lake or stream, the captors and their captive pressed on—almost always at a trot. Whenever Johnny's young legs weakened and he slowed the pace, the braves took turns carrying him on their backs. Just when the boy thought the day would never end, the trail opened up into a clearing by a lake. As the sun was easing behind the trees across the water, the Indians kindled a fire and boiled the turkey eggs they had been carrying all this time. The huge eggs, along with the last of the smoked fish, soothed the hunger pangs. Once again Johnny was made to lie between the father and the older son. Sleep came quickly.

At daybreak a rough hand shook the boy into consciousness. He was still in a daze as his captors hustled him along the trail.

And so one day blended into another. Johnny lost track of time, but he knew more than a week had passed since his capture. Sometime along about the third or fourth day the father noticed that the white boy was limping, and he paused to examine his bruised and swollen feet. That evening he fashioned a pair of crude moccasins from part of his own breech cloth—and they worked. Several times the next day, Johnny pointed to the moccasins and smiled, trying to show his appreciation. But the big Indian never even acknowledged that he understood. Perhaps he didn't want the boy to consider the act as a kindness, rather, something that had to be done to speed the journey.

Travel continued at a torrid pace—usually jogging, slowing to a walk only over the most difficult terrain. Sometimes the trail all but disappeared, but it was always discernable to the Indians. Night brought welcome relief, but the hours of darkness in May were all too few. Food seemed unimportant to the men. The Indians refused to take time to search for something edible, even when Johnny knew they just had to be sharing his sense of starving. Birds' eggs were gathered only when they were stumbled upon or found by a quick search at the end of the day. A not too smart spruce hen was killed with a stick along the trail, a slow moving porcupine was dispatched in the same manner, a couple of late-spawning northern pike were kicked from a shallow stream and a few bull frogs were caught along a lakeshore and harvested for their legs. And one evening the boys pulled and boiled a couple of handsful of tender new cattail sprouts. All the food was surprisingly good; there just wasn't enough of it. Truly these were survival rations.

On the afternoon of the tenth day, although Johnny had really lost count, the Indians quickened their pace. They took turns carrying the 80 pound captive so as to make the best possible time. All this puzzled Johnny. But with the setting sun came the answer: the path suddenly terminated on the banks of a fairly wide river (the Maumee). Although he didn't realize until morning why it was so important they reach the river by nightfall, the truth of the matter was that it was necessary to build a canoe to continue the journey and the Indians wanted a full day in which to do the job.

Up at daybreak, the Indians scattered into the woods, but kept in contact by shouting back and forth to each other. The father, all this time, kept a confused Johnny with him. After a fairly short search, they all gathered at the base of a large hickory tree. The tomahawk the father carried in his belt had an iron axe-head (in contrast to the stone weapons the boys carried). Taking turns and applying their ample muscle, the braves soon felled the tree. Experienced hands stripped the bark from the trunk. Sinewey spruce root and spruce gum were harvested. Sturdy maple limbs were hewed to form ribs and struts and stakes were pounded into the ground to shape the boat. By day's end, a serviceable canoe had been manufactured. The vessel was eased into the water and allowed to soak overnight.

In the morning Johnny was surprised and a little concerned to see the craft almost filled with water, but this didn't seem to bother the Indians in the slightest. The boy didn't know this was all a part of the process of making the boat watertight as the various components were made to swell by soaking. Carefully, they emptied the canoe, slid it back into the water, climbed in and then pushed out into the stream, using paddles they had fashioned around the campfire the night before.

Traveling by water was pure pleasure for the young captive compared to the painful over-land trek he had experienced for so many days. The destination proved to be a small Shawnee settlement on the banks of the river. The whole village seemed to turn out to greet and inspect the travelers. Suddenly, out of the crowd, a young Indian woman leaped at Johnny with a knife in her hand and a blood-curdling scream on her lips. Only a lightning move by the older Indian saved Johnny from death or serious injury. He owed the man his life. But Johnny knew the Indian had only moved to protect him as his possession, not out of any affection or concern for his well being. Of course Johnny had no idea why he had been attacked, but other villagers explained to his captors that the woman's young husband had been killed recently by whites and she was in deep mourning. The incident only served to make the 10-year-old even more apprehensive about what might lie ahead.

Fearing another attempt on the life of their young captive, the kidnappers made their rest stop shorter than they would have liked. So once again they were off. And once again it was cross country, this time in a more northernly direction. Johnny was beginning to wonder if the Indians were lost or if the torturous journey would ever end. Numb—physically and mentally—despair gave way to apathy. But all things, good and bad, do come to an end. The Indians had known exactly what they were doing all along. The kidnapping itself had been carefully planned and executed and the return journey couldn't have been more precise if they had been following a road map, as they headed towards their village which was located on a small body of water close to Lake Huron. The final day saw the party, eager to get home, pushing harder than usual. Johnny sensed something special was ahead, and that afternoon the triumphant trio and their prize sprinted up the path which led to the half-log, half-bark lodge the Indians called "home." Both teenagers let out a whoop as the cabin-like structure came into view. Three children tumbled out of the open door, followed by their very large and very fat mother. Whether Johnny liked it or not—and he didn't—this was his new home.

The huge woman scarcely greeted her husband or sons. Instead she descended on little Johnny—arms outstretched, half laughing, half crying, and jabbering all the way. Still too numb with confusion to comprehend it all, a very tired and very bewildered little boy suddenly found himself enveloped in loving arms and smothered against the ample bosom of this strange woman who was trying her best to mother him. What a complete contrast and surprise the warm reception was to the cold, indifferent, and sometimes cruel treatment he had received from the father and sons.

Greetings over, thoughts turned to food, and soon a fish soup was on the fire. Meanwhile, Johnny found himself the center of attention for the younger children, who were obviously fascinated by his pale complexion and light hair. The boys, about seven and eight years of age, stared in awe. . .speechless. The younger sister was less timid and boldly reached out to touch Johnny. She even stroked his face and hair.

The food was the best that Johnny had eaten since his capture and he gulped down his portion, but when he reached for a second helping the father pushed him back bruskly. His action served notice that so far as he was concerned nothing had changed.

The meal finished, the mother picked up a small bundle and led Johnny up the hillside in back of the lodge; he followed trustingly. The younger children trailed behind. From the higher vantage point, Johnny could see the lake in front of the lodge and other Indian dwellings up the shore. At the height of ground was a small cemetery, and the procession stopped by a fresh grave. The newly cut poles of which the little house was made and the loose earth around it were solemn testimony to a recent death. A stake in the ground on which was crudely carved the shape of a rattlesnake, symbolized the family totem. The big woman sobbed as she untied the mysterious little bundle she carried. Pointing first at the bundle and then at the grave, she indicated that the items belonged to whomever lay beneath the little shelter. Almost reverently she unfolded a small shirt-like garment made of deerskin, and motioned for Johnny to try it on. A pair of moccasins was next, and again she urged the boy to put them on in place of the badly worn, makeshift pair he had been wearing since early in the journey. There was no doubt in Johnny's mind. The grave was surely that of her son, and judging by how well the clothes fit, he must have been about the same age. Now, for the first time, Johnny understood the reason for his kidnapping. He had been chosen to replace the dead son.

The rest of the day, the teenagers who had participated in his capture paraded Johnny around the village, showing off their prize and talking excitedly to their friends about the details of their exploits. But they treated him more like a trophy animal they had shot or a big fish they had caught than like a new brother.

That night, a frightened and still very much bewildered boy lay down to sleep between the fire and the lodge door, being careful not to take anyone else's place. For the first time since his abduction, sleep came slowly, and when it came, it was fitful. Sometime after midnight, the big Indian got up to go outside and stumbled over Johnny in the darkness. Angered, he turned and delivered a hard kick to Johnny's ribs. Even though the brave was barefooted, the blow was severe and the boy's whole chest would ache every time he would sneezed or cough for several weeks.

Morning came slowly, but with it came some surprises and excitement. The whole village gathered together for what appeared to be a festive occasion. Everyone seemed to be in a happy frame of mind. Older men started beating on skin drums as the people came and dancers were soon marking time in an ever-widening circle. Then, to Johnny's amazement, his new mother led him right into the procession of dancers and encouraged him with signs and nods of approval to join in. She was the one friend he seemed to have and he surely didn't want to displease her, so Johnny made up his mind to try to do his best. Watching her every move he attempted to mimic her as he shuffled in time to the rhythm of the drums. By the time the strange looking pair had made their way one full turn around the circle, the boy was matching the big woman step for step. Suddenly, a gift of a small bow and several arrows with blunt wooden heads was thrust into his hands by a bystander. Looking up at his foster mother he was greeted by a broad smile and a flood of meaningless but somehow reassuring words. They danced on, but as they came to the far side of the circle, another stranger snatched the gifts away. Again Johnny looked up in bewilderment; again came the smile and words of reassurance. Next time around another gift was presented, this time some beadwork. And again it was taken away. The ceremony was repeated many times with other gifts of food or clothing or other items. When the village families apparently ran out of gifts, the same items were again presented so that the dance could go on. . .and on. . .and on. The realization sank in. The dance was for him! He was being adopted into the tribe!

"Wow!" Johnny said to himself, over and over again.

Sometime, about half way through the dance, after each gift had been presented a half dozen times or more, a very weary Johnny was allowed to drop out. He chose to sit near the drummers with whom he was greatly fascinated. As he watched the confusion of dancing bodies and listened hypnoticallly to the monotonous drums, Johnny tried to clear his mind and take stock of the situation in which he found himself. It all seemed so unreal, like a dream from which he expected to awaken any second. The kidnapping. . .the weeks of torturous travel . . .and now this, adoption into an Indian family and into the tribe itself. How many times he had dreamed of living with the Indians, even long-ed for that experience, especially on those occasions when he was angry with his father or stepmother. But now he knew he was sorry he had ever made such a wish—really sorry. His new father obviously hated him. He probably had agreed to the kidnapping only to quiet his grieving wife. And the new mother was trying to love him all right, but he didn't know if he could ever love her in return. He couldn't even understand a word she was saying, and she never stopped jabbering. And the rest of the family—he didn't trust either of the older boys any farther than he could throw them, and the young ones he hadn't figured out yet. No doubt about it, he'd gladly trade the whole family for—yes, even for brother Edward. But for now, he'd just have to make the best of it.

Johnny had already lost track of time, but this day of his adoption was his eleventh birthday.

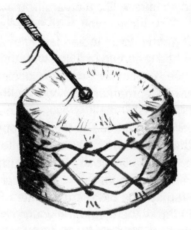

CHAPTER III
TRADED

The only good thing that happened in the weeks that followed was that the big Indian, whom everyone called "Manito-o-geezhik", left on a journey with the two older boys, Kish-kau-ko and Mong-o-zid, along with a half-dozen other men from the village.

"What a relief!" Johnny thought, "No more being kicked, pushed, and shoved around. No more scolding when I reach for seconds. No more being ordered about like a slave by Kish-kau-ko and Mong-o-zid."

But had Johnny known the purpose of their mission, he wouldn't have been so pleased with their departure.

It seems the foster mother, Ozha, was convinced Johnny's father and other whites would some day try to rescue him. She nagged her husband day in and day out until he finally agreed to return to the scene of the kidnapping and kill the father—and others, if necessary. Maybe Manito-o-geezhik was just ready for more adventure; maybe he was afraid Ozha was right and that his own life would then be in jeopardy; or maybe he just wanted to get away from his nagging wife. At any rate, they were on their way.

With the men gone, Johnny was expected to perform many of the chores normally shared by the others. But with the language barrier the boy was still experiencing—and being only 11 years old—things just didn't go very well. The patience of his mother was strained to the breaking point again and again. Even the simple assignment of gathering firewood was not performed satisfactorily. Not knowing better, Johnny was forever bringing in partially rotten limbs or punky popple instead of picking up pine knots or pitch-filled pieces of pine stumps. The mother tried everything to make the boy understand—even whipping him with a willow stick.

The younger brothers laughed at Johnny's many blunders. Even good natured wrestling matches turned into torturous experiences when the two Indian boys—big for their age anyway—discovered that together they could "take" Johnny.

Food was plentiful in summer, and the family's neighbors and relatives were willing to share. Otherwise, they would probably have been pretty hungry much of the time.

All in all, Johnny was one lonely and very unhappy boy, and he knew things would only get worse when Manito-o-geezhik, Kish-kau-ko and Mon-o-zid returned.

Meanwhile, the expedition from the village arrived at their destination on the Kentucky shores of the Ohio River. The scene was the same as when they had left. The preacher-farmer and his son working in the field; the mother busy with her chores around the house and caring for the young ones. Actually, the trip had not been necessary. The Indians had no way of knowing it, but the Tanners had long since given up all hope of finding Johnny on their own. They didn't know even where to begin to search. The rescue party, organized the day of the kidnapping and consisting of John Tanner, son Edward, and a dozen men from the settlement had lost two of their number in the skirmish with the Shawnee raiding party Johnny and his captors had met on the trail. Others had been wounded. No one was anxious to try again. The Tanners had concluded their best hope of ever seeing their son was the possibility of traders or voyageurs running across Johnny and being concerned enough to rescue him or at least tell others about the white boy being raised by Indians.

The braves hid themselves on the edge of the field. They had decided to wait until the father and son worked their way close enough for a sure, noiseless kill with bows and arrows. While waiting, one of the braves from the village observed that Edward Tanner was about the age one of his own sons would have been had he not died of a childhood disease. And so, after a brief discussion, he persuaded the others to try for a second kidnapping! It was not until the next day that Edward was left alone in the field. Stealthily, the Indians crawled down the rows of half-grown corn. The teenager was taken completely by surprise. He didn't even have a chance to cry out. The muzzle loader, which had been at his side ever since Johnny's kidnapping, was only a few feet away, but it may as well have been in the house for all the good it did him. Edward found himself airborn—taken bodily with feet off the ground—into the woods. The kidnappers stopped at a heavy thicket, about three hundred yards in from the field; there they bound the young man hand and foot, gagged him with his own shirt, and tied him to a tree. The Indians left Edward unguarded and returned to the clearing to intercept the father when he returned to the field. But Tanner had seen the war party disappearing into the forest and had taken the rest of his family and fled for help in the opposite direction. About the time the Indians were beginning to grow suspicious over the farmer's long absence, four canoes appeared around the bend in the river, filled with whitemen and bristling with guns. Rushing back to where they had left Edward bound and gagged, they were in for another disappointment—their captive was gone! Only his hat remained on the ground. Miraculously Edward had struggled free. Now, interested only in saving their own lives, the Indians ran deeper into the woods. Manito-o-geezhik slowed down only long enough to swoop up the fallen hat. Weeks later, this was the evidence he presented to young Johnny back in the village to convince him that his entire family had been killed. The ruse worked; the boy was convinced. Sadly, he mused, "No point now in trying to escape. No point in even hoping to be rescued. No family. . . no relatives. . .all they'd do with a kid my age is put him in some orphanage back east. I sure wouldn't like that."

"I'll be better off," Johnny concluded, "just trying to keep alive here with the Indians until I'm older—fifteen, or maybe even fourteen—and then I'll escape. Then I can take care of myself."

Fear of Manito-o-geezhik turned to hate—a hate so bitter that it was eased only when Johnny would tell himself, "Before I go, I'll get even!"

With the father and older brothers home, things went from bad to worse. Even though Johnny was beginning to understand Shawnee, it didn't help all that much. No one showed him how to shoot a bow, in fact, he wasn't even permitted to use the one he had been given during the adoption ceremonies. No one taught him how to set traps or snares. When he tried to follow Kish-kau-ko and Mong-o-zid on their hunting expeditions they would beat him and send him back to the lodge. Helping untangle the nets and laying them out for drying was as near as he got to fishing. All that was left for him to do was women's work—like picking berries or fetching water. He felt clumsy and awkward when he compared himself to the other boys of the village. Oh, he could run as fast as they. Fortunately faster when they were after him, but he envied their grace and quickness and coordination. It was his speed that lead to his being given the name "Shaw-shaw-wa-be-na-see" by his mother. When Johnny finally learned what it meant, he was pleased. He liked being called "Falcon." It would be his Indian name for the rest of his life.

Johnny was envious of the relationship boys his age had with their older brothers and fathers or even with the old men of the village, who taught them so much about hunting, fishing, and trapping and the ways of the wilderness. He had no way of knowing it, but there were those in the village who would gladly have befriended him—but they seemed to feel it would be an insult to the adopting family to do for the boy what his own family chose not to do.

The chores changed with the season. At the end of summer came the wild rice harvest. Again, Johnny was given "squaw's work." He was directed to kneel towards the front of a canoe and beat the loose, ripe kernels out of the heads of the rice as he pulled the long stemmed grain over the boat in front of him. All of the kernels did not ripen at the same time, even in a single head of rice, so the canoes worked the same area every few days until all of the valuable grain was harvested. But Johnny couldn't even do this simple task without getting into trouble. On the third day, as the canoe nosed into some especially heavy rice, a whole flock of mallards flushed into the air within a few feet of him on both sides of the canoe. Scared half to death, Johnny lurched back and in the process upset the narrow boat, dumping Mong-o-zid, the load of rice, and himself into the bottomless ooze that lay just inches below the surface. He was rewarded with one of his more painful beatings and made to stay home, alone, at the lodge—without food. Johnny survived on chokecherries and wintergreen berries he found back in the woods. By this time even his mother wasn't so sure the kidnapping and adoption had been such a good idea.

"Well," Johnny thought, as he tried to ease his hunger pangs with the berries, "things just can't get any worse."

But they did.

One day when the older boys weren't around, Manito-o-geezhik took his white son with him to help build a "blind" from which he hoped to shoot deer at close range with his bow—as they followed a well-used trail down to a meadow where they liked to graze in the evening and drink from a brook. In spite of all his hatred for his foster father, Johnny was happy, almost thrilled that at long last he had been invited to go with the big Indian into the forest and was even intrusted with an important assignment. When Manito-o-geezhik was satisfied that the boy understood what was expected of him (gathering and stacking brush), he walked back to the lodge to sip some rum he had received recently from a crew of voyageurs in return for some fish. The sipping turned to "guzzling" and by the time he returned to the blind to see how Johnny was doing, he was pretty well drunk. He found the job half-done and the tired 11 year old fast asleep. In a rage, he seized the axe-headed tomahawk from his belt and swung with all his might at the sleeping boy's head. Blood poured from the slash and he left him for dead. Returning to the lodge, Manito-o-Geezhik told Ozha what he had done and that he wasn't the least bit sorry. Although her disappointment in her white son had grown, her motherly instincts prevailed and she rushed to the scene, fully expecting to bury the boy. Johnny was still breathing and she carried him to the lodge, sobbing all the way. Having suffered a concussion and the loss of much blood, he didn't regain consciousness for several days, and when he did, Johnny was thoroughly confused. The last thing he could remember was working in the blind. He had no recollection of growing tired and deciding to rest for a few minutes, nor did he know he had fallen asleep. But he did know that he was very sick, and very weak, and had one very sore head.

While the boy was recuperating, Ozha never left him alone with her husband for fear he would decide to finish the job. It was many days before Johnny could be on his feet, and he worried even more than Ozha about that very possibility. He knew there was no way he could escape if Manito-o-geezhik wanted to do him in. Luckily for Johnny, the rum was gone or his fears may have been realized.

Shortly after Johnny was well enough to be up and around, Manito-o-geezhik took off on another journey. Though short in miles, it was to have a profound effect on the white Indian boy's life. The big brave had accumulated a few furs that were already prime and a couple of deer hids which Ozha had scraped and chewed until they were soft and pliable. He heard about a trader who had set up a temporary post on Lake Huron and decided to pay him a visit. When he arrived at the trading post he found a score of other Indians already on hand. Among them was a woman named "Net-no-kwa". She was a remarkable person, with the rank of chief. She had earned the respect of her people, even the men, by her remarkable abilities as a clairvoyant and prophetess. On those occasions she would go into a trance during which she would receive visions of where to find game or would receive wisdom with which to solve vexing problems. Net-no-kwa had her own flag, made from red dress material, which she displayed from the bow of her canoe and which served to identify her in her travels. Even the whitemen respected her—particularly for her position in the tribe and her influence over the other Indians. She was so well known at Fort Mackinac, for example, that the approach of her canoe was routinely honored with a cannon shot.

Manito-o-geezhik was pleased to meet the famous Net-no-kwa and sought to impress her with tales of his exploits, particularly the kidnapping and adoption of his white son. Through these discussions, Net-no-kwa gained the distinct impression that Johnny was for sale, but she wasn't sure whether Manito-o-geezhik's comment that his wife would never part with the boy was true or just said to increase the price. However, she was more than curious. She, too, had lost a son to illness, and since she had only two sons left (and an older, married daughter) the possibility of adopting a new son intrigued her. The first husband had also died, and even though she remarried to a much younger man, she was now too old to have more children. And so she carefully noted the items Manito-o-geezhik selected as well as those he looked at and layed aside. Rum and tobacco topped the list of the items he chose, and a well-decorated comb was among the things he almost traded for; apparently it would have been for his wife. But the comb was too expensive, and he decided to bring Ozha some glass beads instead.

When it came Net-no-kwa's turn to trade, she included some rum—even though she usually did not drink herself—two varieties of tobacco, and the very comb the big Indian had fondled.

As Manito-o-geezhik broke camp, Net-no-kwa casually mentioned that she might be interested in the white boy and that she and her husband just might travel by way of the village.

When Manito-o-geezhik told his wife that he thought it would be a good idea to trade Johnny, she was furious. Nursing the boy back to health had rekindled her love for him and she complained, "Losing my new son would be just as heartbreaking as when my real son died." And then added, "I might just die myself!"

Seeing she would not respond to logic, the big Indian flew into a rage —threatening to kill Johnny then and there.

By the time Net-no-kwa and her party arrived the next day, Ozha was having second thoughts. She feared that sooner or later her husband would make good his threat, and, deep in her heart, she felt the boy would probably never be good for much, even if he fully recovered from the head injury. She just couldn't picture him as a successful hunter or brave warrior. When Net-no-kwa finally made her move and produced the tobacco and nearly a full case of rum, Ozha knew her cause was lost. There was no way Manito-o-geezhik would allow that much liquor and tobacco to escape him. And when the comb was brought out, Ozha's eyes betrayed her desires, and Net-no-kwa had to work hard to suppress a smile of victory.

In a corner of the lodge, Johnny sat through it all in disbelief. He had never dreamed of being sold to another human being. He wondered, "Is this how those black slaves felt when they stepped up on that auction block in Louisville?"

As he fully realized what was happening he concluded, "No wonder Manito-o-geezhik brushed my hair over my scar." It also explained why the big Indian had put new moccasins on Johnny's feet that day, a pair Ozha had made for him while he was sick.

His whole being rebelled at the thought of being sold. "Like a calf!" Johnny mused.

But as Johnny sat there, depressed and feeling very sorry for himself, the realization slowly sank into his battered head that he just might be better off.

The deal completed, Net-no-kwa extended her hand to lead her new possession to the canoe, and Johnny grasped that hand—almost eagerly. Ozha interrupted their departure just long enough to give the boy a half-hearted squeeze. Johnny was a little surprised to see tears tumbling down her cheeks. She was already sorry she had gone along with the trade, but she knew there was no way it could be reversed. For a moment, Johnny felt a little sorry for her.

Manito-o-geezhik just turned his back and walked away, pleased with himself, but not wanting to be around to endure the wailing and complaining he knew would follow.

As Net-no-kwa's canoe moved out onto the lake, Johnny looked with fascination at the flag fluttering from the bow. It gave him a feeling he had been traded to someone special.

Net-no-kwa: No doubt very attractive as a young woman, she was now more handsome than beautiful.

CHAPTER IV
SAULT STE. MARIE

Johnny studied the other occupants of the canoe, his eyes moving from Net-no-kwa to the straight-backed brave in the stern, and then back again to his new mother. Several times, when his eyes met theirs, they would smile and he would quickly look away, embarrassed and unsure how to respond. But he liked Net-no-kwa's easy smile and twinkling eyes. Her appearance was striking. No doubt very attractive as a young woman, she was now more handsome than beautiful. Her sharp features and carefully braided hair added dignity. Johnny was also intrigued by the dozen or so silver ornaments, in the likeness of a beaver, pinned to her deerskin dress, and an equal number of strings of beads of varying lengths and colors worn around her neck, tumbling in an attractive band across her breast. The brave wore his own symbols of wealth—ten brass bracelets on his left arm. Like most eleven year olds, Johnny was a poor judge of the age of adults, but he decided one thing—Net-no-kwa was definitely older than the brave. But what then was their relationship? He was surely too old to be her son—and yet seemed too young to be her husband. While the lad was pondering these things, a canoe pulled out from a point up ahead and waited for them. The two boats drew closer together until they were side by side. Now it was someone else's turn to stare! Two boys in their early teens and a beautiful young Indian woman were in the other canoe, and they just couldn't take their eyes off Johnny as they chatted excitedly with Net-no-kwa and the man in her canoe.

Johnny had learned such Indian words as "Ni-mah-mah" meaning mother, "Nosa" meaning father, and the words for brother and sister: "Ne-kau-nis" and "N'dah-wa-mah". Since the Ottawa tongue which these people spoke was quite similar to Shawnee and had the same basic root words (both were Algonquin tribes), Johnny was able to understand Net-no-kwa when she explained in her soft voice that the young brave in her canoe was her husband, Tau-ga-we-ninne (meaning "great hunter"), that the younger of the teen age boys was Kewatin (meaning "the north wind"), and the older boy was also their son, Wa-me-gon-a-biew (he who puts on feathers). The young woman was identified as O-gay-bow, a second wife of Tau-ga-we-ninne. She was easily the most beautiful Indian maiden the white boy had ever seen. Johnny was a little young to notice such details, but her complexion was flawless and her eyes were round, like a fawn's. He knew that braves frequently took more than one wife—sometimes three or four or as many as they could support. So the fact this brave had two was really no surprise. But he was quite sure Net-no-kwa was the #1 wife—and indeed she was. In fact, it soon became apparent that Net-no-kwa pretty much ran things.

Thus it was, on a nameless lake in an area that would someday be called "Michigan", that Johnny met his new family. Everything happened so fast. It was all so confusing. But Johnny knew one thing—he was glad he had been traded, even if all he was worth was a fancy comb, a couple of plugs of tobacco, and a part of a case of rum!

Conversation and inspection ended, Net-no-kwa's and Tau-ga-we-ninne's canoe took the lead as its prow was turned in a northwesterly direction. The vessels were large (designed for travel on the Great Lakes) and seemed to contain all the family's worldly possessions— and indeed they did. They even had small sails for travel on the open water when the winds were favorable. No one seemed in a hurry, but a steady effort ate up the miles. Camp came early that first day, and Johnny made every effort to help—gathering firewood, fetching water, and lending a hand wherever he could. He tried hard to please.

Gone was the abuse Johnny had suffered at the hands of the first Indian family. Everyone treated him well—even the teenagers. The evening meal finished, the family sat close to the fire to ward off the chill of the early autumn evening. Kewatin, the younger of the boys and only a couple of years older than Johnny, presented him with a crude knife. Johnny couldn't have been more thrilled if it had been silver with a pearl handle! He had not learned any Indian words to express appreciation, but he repeated "thank you" in English over and over again until he remembered the Shawnee word, "o-nish-e-shin", meaning good. Not to be outdone by his younger brother, Wa-me-gon-a-biew produced a little buck-skin pouch with a leather draw string and pressed it into the white boy's hand. Johnny repeated his words of appreciation. And then, fearing his new brothers wouldn't know how good it felt to finally be among friends he gave each of them a quick hug—and everyone laughed.

When Johnny awoke the next day, he watched the women prepare the morning meal but stayed in his blanket. Mist was rising off the water and flocks of ducks shuttled back and forth on the way to their first feeding. The rays of the rising sun accented the few maple leaves that had already turned red and orange. There was a crispness in the air that foretold of colder mornings to come. The fire felt good.

The charm of the September morning was broken by Net-no-kwa's demand that everyone be up and about. Johnny was slow to roll out and Wa-me-gon-a-biew manfully lifted the white boy, blanket and all, staggered to the water's edge, and made believe he was going to throw him in. Johnny protested loudly—half laughing, half screaming—until his red brother finally set him on his feet on dry ground. He loved it!

The family broke camp at a leisurely pace—in complete contrast to the hurried travel he had experienced following his kidnapping. To his delight, Johnny was allowed to ride in the canoe with his new brothers, and they couldn't have been prouder or more pleased to have him. Feeling wanted, Johnny was more at ease and he asked a million questions. Kewatin and Wa-me-gon-a-biew almost competed to answer them as the boys struggled to overcome the language barriers.

"Where is your village?" Johnny began.

"We used to live on the shores of Lake Huron, not far from where we found you."

"Used to?"

"Yes—we are moving west."

"How far west?" asked Johnny, "Where are we headed?"

"To the land of the Assineboin, to the Lake of Dirty Water (Winnipeg) and perhaps even farther west to Clearwater or even Athabasca. We will travel until we reach the relatives of our father."

"How long will all this travel take?"

"We do not know—many moons."

"Will we be there before the lakes freeze?"

"Oh, my, no!" Kewatin responded, "**Many** moons. We will spend the winter at the great village of the Ojibway (Sault Ste. Marie).

"Next winter we may spend on The Lake of the Sand Hills (Big Traverse Bay of Lake of the Woods)," Wa-me-gon-a-biew added.

"Why do we travel so far?"

"We are going to the land of buffalo—a land of many beaver—a land filled with fisher, marten, otter, mink, and all kinds of animals whose fur we will trade for all sorts of good things. The animals have been all trapped out near our old village."

The major questions answered, Johnny sought to learn more about his new family. He was assured Net-no-kwa was indeed considerably older than Tau-ga-we-ninne (by about 17 years older). But the boys did not know why O-gay-bow had no children.

"Has Net-no-kwa been married before?" Johnny pried.

"Yes, but her first man died in battle against the Roaster Indians (Sioux)."

"Did she have any children with her first husband?"

"Yes, our older half sister, Win-et-ka. She is married and has two little girls of her own." Kewatin explained, "We will meet them at Rainy Lake and take them with us. They have gone ahead to visit relatives of her husband—an Ojibway."

"Is Tau-ga-we-ninne a great Hunter?"

"The greatest," both boys replied, almost in unison.

"Kewatin, how many deer have you killed?"

"Many."

"How many?" Wa-me-gon-a-biew teased.

"Well, two by myself, but I have helped kill others!" the younger Indian replied.

"How many have you killed then?" Johnny pressed the older boy.

"More than Kewatin, that's for sure, and I've killed a bear!"

"Oh, sure," Kewatin admitted, "but it was still in its den."

"Has Tau-ga-we-ninne killed other braves from enemy tribes?"

"Two—that is why he wears two feathers."

"Has he killed any white men?" Johnny asked with hesitation and a touch of concern in his voice.

"No," came the reassuring reply from Kewatin.

Then Wa-me-gon-a-biew again teased, "At least not lately!"

Questions followed about lakes, streams, and the wilderness in general—questions Johnny's first Indian family had ignored. Questions about Indian names for partridges, ducks, and all varieties of animals. Asking and answering these questions was like a game, because the Indian boys did not know the English words and Johnny had to do his best to describe each with Shawnee words and signs.

Questions about how and where to hunt and trap were deferred with the promise, "We'll show you," or "Tau-ga-we-ninne will teach you."

Day blended into day as the family continued to the northwest—sometimes across lakes, often down rivers, and too often across overland portages. Frequently they met other Indians who stopped to visit; Johnny was always a center of attention. Once while traveling on Lake Michigan, a brigade of four canoes of voyageurs was sited. The boys urged their new brother to hide so that they would not take him from them. Had Johnny realized that his own family was still alive, he would have at least been tempted to attract the whites' attention, but he was certain they were dead and the very thought of ending up in an orphanage back east made him shudder. So Johnny gladly lay in the bottom of the canoe until the voyageurs were well out of sight.

The family's fear of encountering whites caused Johnny to have his first really unpleasant experience since being sold to Net-no-kwa. After reaching the western end of Lake Huron the first stop of significance was to be Mackinac, the famous island fort and trading post. Net-no-kwa had been there many times and was well known by the traders. She knew that once the soldiers recognized the red flag in the prow of her canoe, a cannon would be fired in her honor. She wanted very much to impress Johnny with her acceptance by white men, but she feared missionaries or others might insist Indians had no right to raise a white child. So with genuine reluctance, the canoes put to shore on the mainland at a cabin across from the island, a cabin built by whites but now occupied by an Ottawa family known to Net-no-kwa. After a brief visit and assurances to Johnny that they would return for him the next day, the family departed for Mackinac. Johnny was treated well enough until the next morning, when the host family decided to check their nets but didn't want to take Johnny along in case he would try to run away. So they decided to lock him in a sort of root cellar under the house for safe keeping. He was reluctant to enter the cellar but felt he had little choice; he knew if he struggled or protested he would be the loser. The tiny room was totally dark and as the sounds of departing feet died away, Johnny was petrified with fear. His mind played all sorts of tricks on him and he was certain the hole was shared with rats and snakes or worse. When he heard absolutely nothing and no harm had came to him, his thoughts turned to other fears, like, "Maybe my family won't come back!"

"I sure wouldn't want to live with this new family. People who lock a kid in a cellar probably wouldn't treat you very nice."

"Maybe a storm will come up and everybody will drown! I'll die here," he thought.

But after a few horrible hours, Johnny heard footsteps and voices as Net-no-kwa called, "Shaw-shaw-wa-be-na-se!"

He thought it was the most beautiful voice he had ever heard. With a loud cry he announced his where-abouts. In seconds, they were reunited.

Net-no-kwa and Tau-ga-we-ninne were furious with the family for locking Johnny in the cellar and leaving him in the first place. Wa-me-gon-a-biew wanted to ambush the family when they returned and kill them all! Kewatin suggested burning the cabin down. But since everything had worked out all right and they might never see these people again anyway, the adults ignored both suggestions and returned to their canoes for the short distance left to the head of the lake and Sault Ste. Marie.

As the family made camp that night, Johnny had a suggestion, "Let's not worry about any white men we may meet. I'll tell them the truth—all my old family are dead and you are my new family and I want very much to stay with you."

Net-no-kwa gave her fair-haired son a hug and agreed, "We will no doubt meet other whites on the trail, sometimes unexpectedly when they cannot be avoided. Your plan is a good one."

The days had grown shorter and colder, and the family were pleased they were almost at their destination for the winter. There was much work to be done. The lodge had to be set up; new mats woven, fish netted and smoked, trap lines established, etc. The very morning the first fingers of ice were noticed in the rushes by shore was the day they arrived at the great village of the Ojibway.

Johnny was impressed. He had never seen so many Indians in one place (probably close to 1000). There were bark and skin lodges for as far as he could see. He learned, however, that the village was once considerably larger (in the 1600's) when the Ojibway made it their capital during the years following their exodus from the east, after being defeated in a blood bath at the hand of the Iroquois. Thousands of their people had died because of the superior weapons of the enemy. Now, he was told, larger concentrations of Ojibway could be found at La Pointe (on an island off the Wisconsin shores of Lake Superior) and on Rainy Lake. However, La Pointe, too, had passed its peak of influence as the Chippewa moved on into Minnesota and Ontario in the 1700's.

At first, Johnny was a little apprehensive being among so many Indians—remembering the woman who had attacked him shortly after his kidnapping, but his fears proved unnecessary. Although nearly everyone considered him as a curiosity, no one seemed interested in doing him harm. A couple of times when boys were inclined to tease him or say anything unpleasant, Kewatin and Wa-me-gon-a-biew were right there to defend him. "What a difference," he thought, "from the way I was treated in the first village."

Net-no-kwa, Tau-ga-we-ninne, and O-gay-bow found a few families they knew, and with their help sought out the village leadership, who made them welcome. With winter threatening, Tau-ga-we-ninne and his Indian sons joined with other men from the village in fishing and hunting expeditions, but Johnny was assigned to the lodge to help the women. At first he resented doing "squaw's work", but everyone assured him, "Next year it will be different," and he felt better.

Besides, there was a boy about his age in the lodge next door with whom he could play and explore when time permitted, and Net-no-kwa saw to it that there was time each day. His new friend, Wa-bo-se, had a good supply of fire-hardened clay balls and stone marbles, with which they improvised many a contest, and there were also other toys and games. Rushes were woven into rings that were tossed in a contest much like horseshoe; there were endless games of tag, hide and seek, and follow the leader. And on rainy days the mothers showed the boys how to cut out figures and designs from birch bark. They also watched the older boys and young men of the village play lacrosse and tried a hand at it themselves when the equipment was not in use. With the coming of snow, the boys joined other village youth in sliding down hills while balancing with one foot on a miniature toboggan about 4 inches wide and 3 or 4 feet long; a cord was attached to the tip to help steer and keep balance.

Wa-bo-se was also the proud owner of his own bow and a set of blunt, wooden-headed arrows. Together, they practiced their shooting almost daily. The boys were warned not to go far from the village, but it was a proud day when Johnny returned to the lodge with a fat, bushy-tailed grey squirrel he had tumbled out of an oak tree. Net-no-kwa announced that she would clean it for her hunter-son and that the feast of first fruits (called "Ostenetahgawin") would be held in his honor. Kewatin and Wa-me-gon-a-biew were kind enough not to tease their white brother about the size of his first trophy, but instead tried to outdo each other in praising Johnny for his achievement at so young an age (especially for a white boy). Everyone predicted, with tongue in cheek, that he would surely become a great hunter!

The winter was a pleasant one for the family. Although food was not abundant, there was always enough. Tau-ga-we-ninne was assigned an area for trapping, but being a new family (and Ottawa at that), his trap line was quite far from the village and he and the older boys often spent nights away from the lodge in a little shelter made of cedar boughs laid over a structure formed by bent poplar poles. Spruce branches, piled thick and high, made a comfortable bed.

Johnny found it difficult to accept the fact that his Indian brothers were more mature and experienced and that he had to remain at home. But there came a time, early in March, when the worst of the winter was over and the bitter cold was gone for another year, when Tau-ga-we-ninne announced, "Tomorrow, my little Falcon, we will take you trapping with us."

Johnny was beside himself with excitement. He hugged Wa-me-gon-a-biew and tried to wrestle Kewatin to the ground, but soon found himself bottom boy in a happy pile up of arms and legs. Johnny did not sleep that night—not one wink.

When morning finally came, Net-no-kwa sent the male members of her family happily on their way with their stomachs warmed by her favorite fish broth. The snow had started to melt but a good crust had formed over-night during the lower temperatures, helping their snowshoes to work well. Since Johnny weighed less than 100 lbs., he was able to scamper ahead, almost never breaking through the crust, but he was a funny sight with his oversized, clumsy, webbed snowshoes.

The sun had passed its zenith when Tau-ga-we-ninne called a halt to share some jerky and explain to Johnny that the first trap was just ahead—a mink-set on a small stream. He related how a log had been thrown across the creek, with a chunk hacked out of it near its mid-point so that when a trap was set in this spot, it would be under water and there would be no human scent; the rest of the log was above the surface. In this manner, a mink might choose to swim through the opening and hopefully would step on the trap and be caught. The trap was chained to the log so that the animal would drown. The rest-stop completed, the hunting party proceeded to the stream. As the log came into view, the father gave a little cry of triumph and pointed to the cut-away portion—the trap was out of sight. Tau-ga-we-ninne urged his foster son to pull on the chain. Johnny needed little encouragement and pulled so hard the sleek, black mink—very much drowned—came flying out of the water.

Within seconds the trap was re-set and the party was on its way to the next stop—where the carcass of a mink had been staked out near a fox trail with traps set under the snow on either side. As they approach-ed Johnny could hear an animal threshing around in the brush; ap-parently it had smelled the trappers as they drew near. Johnny's heart was beating so fast and so loudly he though it would come up into his throat! Then he saw it. . .the most beautiful. . .the deepest red. . .the longest tailed. . .the biggest fox he had ever seen. Since it was still alive, Tau-ga-we-ninne took the tomahawk from his belt and quickly dispat-ched it with a single blow.

Although he carried a rifle and his oldest son was custodian of the family's muzzle-loaded hand gun, Tau-ga-we-ninne preferred to save his powder and shot for hunting. Besides, there was less chance he would damage the fur. Kewatin was responsible for a bow and a supply of arrows just in case a more dangerous animal was found in a trap—such as a wolf or wolverine. Inasmuch as the father and sons checked their trap line regularly and frequently, animals were usually found alive. In this way there was less chance they would get away or if they should die in the trap, it was less likely ravens or predators would ruin the hide.

The next three sets were snares tied to trees above well-worn trails—but all were empty. Then came a small spruce and cedar swamp which was criss-crossed with dozens of rabbit trails. Because the women and boys of the village had snared-out most of the rabbits near there, Kewatin and Wa-me-gon-a-biew had set a dozen or more snares in the swamp—as much for food as for fur. Excitedly, they ran from one to the other, each urging Johnny, "Come with me!"

When the turmoil was over, Kewatin was triumphant. He proudly showed off two, all-white snow shoes and a smaller, gray cottontail, Wa-me-gon-a-biew didn't have much to say; he had a single rabbit to show for his efforts. As the afternoon wore on the trapline yielded another red fox and a fisher. Johnny mistakenly identified it as, "The biggest mink I ever saw," and was appropriately teased for not knowing the difference. A covey of partridges was spotted by Kewatin in a poplar thicket. He inched his way as close as he dared and managed to pick off two of them before they flew. Johnny was impressed, but Wa-me-gon-a-biew, a typical older brother, snorted, "Huh, it took you six arrows and you even lost one of those!"

Then, shortly before dusk, came the beaver ponds with their huge, ice-bound lodges—located behind dams along a winding stream. Beaver pelts were among the most valuable, but they were also among the more difficult animals to trap in winter. Breaking into a frozen lodge that time of the year was virtually impossible, so a hole had to be chopped in the ice. A poplar pole (its bark is a favorite delicacy of the beaver) was then driven through the hole into the bottom of the pond. Traps were secured to the pole, and when a beaver set one off, the animal was quickly drowned. Sets out of the water in spring or autumn were easier to set and tend, but had to be checked regularly so that an animal would not chew off his foot. Because Tau-ga-we-ninne did not have an unlimited number of traps, he supplemented his beaver sets with huge, hand-forged trebble hooks, tied under water near the lodge entrance. These could easily tangle in the animal's fur and also cause quick drowning. All of these things Johnny learned as he followed excitedly from lodge to lodge. By the time they reached their over-night shelter, three beaver—one of them huge—had been added to the collection.

A fire was built and Johnny was assigned the responsibility for feeding it. Tau-ga-we-ninne produced a kettle he had brought to the shelter on an earlier visit and sent Kewatin to fill it from the last hole they had chopped in the ice. Two big hands full of wild rice were thrown into the kettle as the water was brought to a boil. Meanwhile, Wa-me-gon-a-biew dressed out a rabbit and the two partridges. These were broiled over the fire on "green" sticks until they were nearly done. Then they were cut into small pieces and added to the rice. Everyone was so hungry they could hardly wait—but the meal was well worth the delay and eventually the four trappers ate their fill.

After the hearty supper, the father and his Indian sons skinned out their day's bag. Johnny watched with fascination and tried to help first one and then the other by holding the animal as the skinner pulled and cut the pelt away from the carcass. He couldn't remember ever being so tired—even while on the torturous run with his kidnappers. But he wouldn't give up until the last animal was finished. All of the pelts were wrapped together in a pack to help prevent freezing, because they would be stretched on wooden frames (fur side in) by Net-no-kwa and O-gay-bow when they returned to the village. By the time Tau-ga-we-ninne stuffed the last fur in the pack, all three boys were fast asleep, huddled together for warmth under their blankets on top of the bouncy spruce boughs.

The next day was spent following a trail that made a loop over hills, across streams, through swamps, along the shore of a small lake, and back to the shelter by dark. It was a productive day: six beaver pelts,

Red River it was decided to carry the boy on a blanket rather than wait and have to make the journey alone through a strange land. Everyone was certain Kewatin would be able to walk in a few days, anyway. Tau-ga-we-ninne was well enough to lift a corner of the stretcher with his good arm, but was unable to carry a pack because of his wound. It was in this manner that the family worked its way up the long, nine-mile portage to Pigeon River. Spunk Wood, who was also in the procession and feeling badly that he had caused Tau-ga-we-ninne's wound, helped tote some of the family's possessions and even took a turn helping carry Kewatin.

Because the canoes they had used on the Great Lakes (called Mackinacs by the Indians) were too large and cumbersome to handle on portages, they had been sold at the trading post. So when they reached Fort Charlotte on the Pigeon River, Tau-ga-we-ninne, Wa-me-gon-a-biew and Net-no-kwa began building two smaller vessels. Meanwhile, Johnny and O-gay-bow were sent back to Grand Portage for the remainder of the family's possessions. They stayed overnight and were half way back to the river, when they met Wa-me-gon-a-biew. He began to cry and blurted out, "Our father is dying and wants to see both of you!" They took off on a run.

Shortly after Johnny and O-gay-bow had left the day before, Tau-ga-we-ninne had suddenly became very ill and had a premonition he would not recover. His first thought was to kill Spunk Wood who had given him the wound. Using his good arm he grabbed his rifle and staggered out of the temporary lodge the family was using. He found Sug-gut-tau-gun sitting by his own shelter but before he could fire, Kewatin cried out, "Don't Father, if I was well I could help you kill this man and could help protect our family from vengeance of his friends after he is dead, but see how sick I am. I, too, may be about to die! My brothers are still young and weak and we shall all be murdered if you kill Spunk Wood!"

Dazed, Tau-ga-we-ninne turned to Kewatin and said, "My son, I love you too much to refuse you." With that, he let his gun fall to the ground and slowly made his way back to the shelter.

When Johnny, O-gay-bow and Wa-me-gon-a-biew came into view of the lodge where Tau-ga-we-ninne lay, they heard Kewatin crying and Net-no-kwa wailing. The fallen brave lay very still; his eyes were open, but he was unable to speak. As Johnny knelt beside him, Tau-ga-we-ninne was able to lay his hand across his adopted son's wrist. He spoke his love with his eyes and then died.

Net-no-kwa was determined to bury her husband back at Grand Portage. She purchased a wooden casket from the traders at Fort Charlotte and, with the help of several other Indians—including Spunkwood—undertook the sad journey back to Lake Superior. Kewatin insisted on going along. His knee was less painful at that moment and he said he could walk if he leaned on Johnny. But before they reached Grand Portge, he once again had to be carried on his blanket. At one point, the entourage stopped to rest and Kewatin, overcome by grief, pulled his knife and would have stabbed Spunkwood from behind and probably killed him, but Wa-me-gon-a-biew pushed his arm back down and sadly asked, "What good will it do? His family is large; his friends are many. They will surely kill us all."

Tau-ga-we-ninne was buried in a white man's cemetery, a credit to the prestige and influence of his wife. Although as sad as if he had lost his white father, Johnny was enthralled with the ceremony. Tau-ga-we-ninne's body was wrapped in heavy birchbark before being placed in the wooden box Net-no-kwa had purchased from the traders. His pipe, some tobacco, his brass arm rings, and some food and utensils were laid in the casket beside him. Johnny learned later that these were to sustain him during the four day journey to the Happy Hunting Ground—where all his needs would be provided. Family members spoke to Tau-ga-wa-ninne—as though he were right there—urging him to be careful as he traveled. The body was lowered into the grave with the feet facing west. Net-no-kwa then began a slow dance around the open grave, accompanied by a single drum. When it was all over, she planted one of her flags at graveside.

The following day, the family and their friends made the return trip to Fort Charlotte and continued building canoes. When all was ready, the caravan resumed the journey to the Red River. Johnny and O-gay-bow carried most of the family possessions in their canoe, while Net-no-kwa and Wa-me-gon-a-biew took Kewatin with them. The injured boy lay in the bottom of the boat most of the time and complained that he was now "sick all over". It was a struggle to carry Kewatin over the portages. Those bearing him sank deeply into the muddy spots. Scraggly bushes reached out and tried to catch their ankles, and mosquitoes tormented them, seeming to know their victims had their hands full and could not defend themselves. When they arrived at Moose Lake, Kewatin felt so poorly he begged, "Let me die here." Net-no-kwa and O-gay-bow talked it over and agreed they should not go on, but stay here until Kewatin recovered. It was with great sorrow and heavy hearts that the family watched the canoes of their friends cross the lake and one by one

Kewatin

disappear from their view.

At least the setting where they stopped was beautiful, and Johnny told his mother that he thought the water was as clear as Lake Superior.

While Net-no-kwa and O-gay-bow constructed a lodge, Johnny and Wa-me-gon-a-biew unpacked the gill net the family had traded for at Mackinac. One end was secured to the shore and the other pulled out into the lake by canoe as far as the net would stretch. A good sized rock was tied to the bottom corner of the far end of the net and dropped in the lake to anchor it. Little bags filled with small stones were tied all along the bottom edge, holding the net against the bottom of the lake so fish could not swim under it. Small wooden floats along the upper edge stretched the net towards the surface to cover a maximum area. A large float was tied to the far end to mark the spot.

The next morning it was scarcely daylight when Johnny shook Wa-me-gon-a-biew and said, "Let's go see what we've caught."

A typical teenager, he pushed his white brother away with a gruff, "Go back to sleep; it's too early."

But Johnny stayed up and hunkered by the lake's edge, listening to the wilderness come to life. From the woods across the water, came the hoot of a great horned owl—ready to go to sleep after a night of hunting. Down the shore to the left he could hear a hen mallard clucking contentedly as her half-grown brood made their own noises, somewhere between a peep and a quack. Song birds chirped in the bushes behind the lodge. A light breeze off the lake kept the mosquitoes from spoiling the charm of the wilderness dawn.

Wa-me-gon-a-biew got thinking about the net, and reluctantly decided he might as well get up. The boys paddled out towards the marker. The plan was to turn the canoe parallel to the shore and then pull the net across the topside of the boat. As the fish were removed—and hopefully there would be some—the empty net would then be allowed to slide back into the water on the far side, thus resetting it. Meanwhile, the canoe would be pulled sideways towards shore until all of the net had been checked. Each boy was armed with a pick (a hand-forged nail point protruding from a wooden handle) with which the net openings could be stretched so that the fish which had been caught by their gills could be removed.

As they approached, the marker buoy began to dance. When the canoe was in place the boys proceeded to pull the net—it was heavy and obviously "alive" with fish! First came a walleye, then a whitefish, then a trout, and another, and another. Luckily the openings were only about 4 inches when stretched (thus limiting the size of the fish) or they would never have held them all in the boat! By the time they had moved the full length of the net, the boys found themselves sharing the canoe with about 80 trout, whitefish, walleyes, and northerns. The commotion awakened the rest of the family and by the time they touched shore, Net-no-kwa was waiting. Although delighted, she suggested the boys take up the net, because they now had far more fish than they could use, even after smoking and drying them.

The woods around Moose Lake abounded with game. With their father gone and Kewatin critically ill, Johnny asked that he be allowed to carry the second rifle, but Net-no-kwa was hesitant. A compromise was finally reached and Johnny was entrusted with the hand gun. The woman charged her older son with the responsibility for teaching his white brother how to use it safely. However, the mischievous Wa-me-gon-a-biew gave the muzzle loader a nearly double portion of powder and then suggested, "We don't want to waste our powder and shot by shooting at a target; let's find a partridge or pigeon and see what kind of a hunter I have for a brother!"

"You bet!" was Johnny's eager reply, and the boys were off. It took a while but in due time a whole flock of passenger pigeons was spotted in a clump of willows. Wa-me-gon-a-biew stood back while Johnny carefully sneaked within range. What happened next Johnny would never forget, and the very thought of it made him flinch every time he pulled a trigger for the next month. The handgun went off with a roar and flew back, out of his hand, hitting him in the forehead! Johnny went on his back in shock. Wa-me-gon-a-biew casually walked over, stared down at his fallen brother, and asked with a grin, "Are you still too small and too weak to be a hunter?"

Johnny was about to cry—more from humiliation than pain—when he heard the flapping of the wings of a bird on the ground. "I got him!" he yelled, and was on his feet and retrieved the pigeon in a bound.

Back in camp, Wa-me-gon-a-biew confessed all and Kewatin, sick as he was, laughed until he cried. Net-no-kwa didn't think it was funny at all. She put both hands on her hips, as was her custom when she was angry, and reprimanded, "Don't you know that you could have blown up the gun or even killed Shaw-shaw-wa-be-na-se?"

When Wa-me-gon-a-biew finally admitted the seriousness of his prank, Net-no-kwa proclaimed, "Tonight we must celebrate the feast of Ostenetahgawin in honor of my son's first bird. Now go back into the bush and shoot some more."

The boys needed no further encouragement and returned a couple of hours later with three partridges and three more pigeons, taking turns shooting the hand gun. That night, as the feast of first fruits was celebrated, Net-no-kwa made certain Johnny had his first bird as his very own to eat. But a couple of times when Net-no-kwa turned her back, Wa-me-gon-a-giew pointed at the egg-sized bump on his brother's forehead and snickered. Johnny said nothing, but later that evening when his big brother lay by the fire with his back turned, he pounced on him and pinned his shoulders to the ground. Wa-me-gon-a-biew laughed until his sides hurt and graciously let Johnny get his revenge.

As fall progressed and furs came into prime, Wa-me-gon-a-biew and Johnny began trapping. They worked the area together because the younger boy was not yet strong enough to spring the heavier traps. They remembered most of what Tau-ga-we-ninne had taught them, but their efforts weren't nearly as productive as when he was living. Yet, day by day, they piled up an impressive store of beaver, otter, mink and muskrat skins. The latter they found in a grassy slough about a mile in back of the lodge. Muskrats were relatively easy to trap—in their houses, on their runways and on their feeder stations. Net-no-kwa and O-gay-bow did most of the skinning and stretching.

The women also gathered rice, but the crop was poor due to high water earlier in the year. However, that which they harvested was carefully processed. First the rice was dried on sheets of birchbark. Then it was parched (but not burned) in a kettle to further loosen the husks. The separation was completed by pounding or trampling with clean moccasins. It was then winnowed by tossing it into the air on a windy day; the husks were blown away and only the heavier kernels remained.

As the signs of the coming of winter became more ominous, Net-no-kwa proclaimed one night, "We must return to Grand Portage. When the snow comes and the bitter cold sets in, it is possible that we could starve. And there is no one within miles to help us if we are in need—neither white nor Indian.

Of course, she was also concerned about Kewatin, who had both good days and bad. Sometimes he was even able to be up and hobble around camp. Net-no-kwa had tried all the appropriate herbs and roots of medicinal value she could find. She made a brew from balsam needles, tea from catnip, boiled leaves from the yarrow plant, and prepared a broth from the root of Joe Pye weed. But all to no avail. She confided to the others, "Kewatin will never live through the winter if we experience any hardships."

Thus it was that when Kewatin had his next good day, the family headed back east. A few days later, when they reached Fort Charlotte on the Pigeon River, Kewatin grew worse and had to be once again carried on his blanket over the long trail. But they made it, and before the first snow, they were settled in for the winter at Grand Portage.

With the coming of the cold, Kewatin's health continued to deteriorate. One of the white traders from the fort, who was reputed to know something about medicine, came to look at the boy. He said, however, he really didn't know what to do unless it would be to amputate the infected leg, but he was pretty sure the boy was too weak to survive the shock of so drastic a remedy—so he did nothing. Within the month, Kewatin died. The ground was frozen only an inch or two, and he was buried next to his father. Net-no-kwa placed another of her flags at the graveside. She mourned the loss of her son for many days, and could frequently be found between the graves of Tau-ga-we-ninne and Kewatin, where she wept and cried out loud. She nearly despaired, and not without good reason. After all, she had lost two husbands and two sons, and the two remaining boys were really too young to provide for the family. The future looked bleak as she wondered, "What will go wrong next?"

Although Johnny and Wa-me-gon-a-biew were both more resilient than their mother, the death of Kewatin was their first thought every morning and often their last thought at night. Johnny was perhaps even more despondent than Wa-me-gon-a-biew over the death of Kewatin. To the white boy, Kewatin was more than a brother, he was his best friend. It wasn't long, however, before their minds were occupied more with concerns for survival and questions about the future. The double tragedy matured both of them, and they accepted their responsibilities for the welfare of the diminishing family with the absolute confidence of youth.

Johnny was perhaps a little less concerned about the future than the older brother; he had been bounced around so much in the past two years he was unconsciously beginning to accept tragedy and heartache as part of life. But the two deaths in the once happy family did draw the boys and their mother closer together. As for O-gay-bow, she was well liked by all, but with the passing of Tau-ga-we-ninne, was thought of more as a friend than family. It wasn't long before she announced that she was going to live with a brother-in-law and his family where she would not be a burden.

As the days grew shorter and colder, game became more scarce and trapping proved almost totally non-productive. Most of the animals had been shot out or trapped out near the fort. That is why Johnny and Wa-me-gon-a-biew decided to establish an over-night shelter one day's journey from Grand Portage, and hunt from there. It was on one of these expeditions when everything that could go wrong did, and further tragedy was narrowly avoided.

The "spike camp" was made of cedar boughs laid over a frame of curved poplar poles, just as Tau-ga-we-ninne had taught them, and spruce boughs were used for bedding. After several trips, the heat from the camp fire had dried the needles until an almost explosive condition existed. That particular day, the hunting had gone poorly. The boys missed the only game they had seen—a caribou across a valley. Dead tired and discouraged, they had a skimpy supper and then curled around the fire. Soon both fell into a deep sleep. Sometime in the night the fire apparently hit a deposit of pitch in one of the pine logs and the flames leaped high enough to ignite the tinder dry cedar boughs. The whole shelter ignited almost instantaneously. Parts of the boys' clothing caught fire, but they had the presence of mind—even though awakened from a deep sleep—to roll in the the snow, putting out the flames.

With the coming of daylight they headed home. On the way it was necessary to cross a fairly fast river with treacherous ice. First Wa-me-gon-a-biew broke through, then, before Johnny could throw himself flat on the ice, he too fell in. With snowshoes on their feet, it was especially difficult to stay afloat, but they finally managed to get over on their backs with their snowshoes held against the current. With the help of their elbows and with the current pushing on their feet, they managed to work themselves back up onto the ice. As they gingerly crossed the remainder of the stream, the bitter cold froze their jackets and leggings stiff as boards. Numb fingers tugged at the lacings on their snowshoes and they finally came off. The boys dug in their packs for punk wood with which to start a fire, but it was soggy wet. Panic stricken, Wa-me-gon-a-biew looked at Johnny and through clenched, chattering teeth mumbled, "This is the end for both of us," and with that, lay down in the shelter of the river bank and tried to curl up.

Johnny stared down at the older boy in disbelief, then yelled, "No! No! No!" and kicked him as hard as he could.

Wa-me-gon-a-biew muttered, "Forget it little brother," and turned his back.

"We're not going to die! We're not going to die!" Johnny screamed and jumped on top of his brother, pummeling him with both fists.

Finally, Wa-me-gon-a-biew responded and they rolled over and over wrestling in the snow until both boys were panting and actually sweating from exertion. "All right," Wa-me-gon-a-biew said, letting Johnny up, "Now we'll find some dry wood."

An old pine log lay on the bank and it was the immediate object of the boys' attack—kicking it apart until the dry, rotted wood was exposed. To this they added tiny pieces of birchbark. Johnny formed a windbreak with his hands while Wa-me-gon-a-biew struck his flint and steel. The first spark caught! Soon they had a roaring fire going and before long their clothing was dry and comfortable. Exhausted from the ordeals of the past twenty-four hours, the boys were content to remain by the fire and spend the night there. The following morning, they headed for home at the "crack of dawn", happy and grateful to be alive. Along the way they met their mother coming up the trail. Net-no-kwa said that when they were over-due, she had a premonition something was wrong, and she carried both food and clothing. It was a happy ending to an unhappy hunt.

As the winter went on, hunting grew even worse. The family was approaching starvation conditions. Then one day a stranger came to their lodge. He was a swamp Indian or "Muskegee"; his name was Pot-wan-we-ninne, meaning "the Smoker." He said he had heard of their plight at the fort and invited them to return with him to his lodge at Burntwood River, some two days travel to the west. "My own family is small," Pot-wan-we-ninne said, "With the boys' help I can easily provide for your needs."

He further promised to bring them back to Grand Portage in the spring, so they could continue their journey west if they so desired.

Net-no-kwa considered the offer as inspired by the Great Spirit and quickly accepted. The rest of the winter the family wanted for nothing. The boys even stockpiled some furs for trading back at the fort.

Such was the kindness of the Indians at that time for those in need. For the rest of their lives, Johnny and Wa-me-gon-a-biew would consider members of the Smoker's family as brothers and sisters, and would treat them accordingly.

CHAPTER VI
ISLE ROYAL

Springtime in the wilderness is in itself an adventure. Even before the snow is off the ground the sap begins to run in the maple trees—an assurance to the Indian that the dangers of starvation are past. Then, as the ice melts along the shores of the lakes, northern pike—some as large as posts—make wakes in the water like alligators as they nose their way through the weeds and water grasses in their annual spawning ritual. The first ice-free water also means the spectaculor return of ducks, geese and other waterfowl—all at their peak of color—darting in and out along the shoreline in their mating flights. In the woods the receding snow is followed by blades of grass, bright green against the background of last fall's dead leaves, bringing deer and other vegetarians out from their winter hiding places. In the south, spring is a gradual process, sometimes unnoticed. But in the wilderness of the north, spring makes a dramatic and sudden appearance. You can see it, you can smell it, you can feel it in the air. For Johnny, Net-no-kwa and Wa-me-gon-a-biew, the spring of 1793 was promise of an easier and hopefully happier life than the tragic months that had brought the previous year to a close.

Before returning to Grand Portage, the little family joined "the Smoker" and his people in traveling two days' journey south to the sugarbush camp to manufacture maple sap products. The bark of each maple tree was slashed and a cedar splint driven in to serve as a spout for the sap—which dripped steadily, day and night, into birchbark baskets. Everyone joined in gathering the sap and dumping it into huge iron kettles where it boiled leisurely for days and days over an open fire until it was reduced to about 1/40th of its original volume and became syrup. Although some of the syrup was used in that form, most of it was poured into basswood troughs where it was gently stirred until it became granulated, thus forming sugar. Some of the syrup was poured into smaller molds and allowed to harden into a candy-like consistancy. Maple sugar could also be stirred into water, thus making a beverage, and it was used extensively as seasoning in a great variety of dishes.

While in the sugarbush camp, the family stayed in a fairly large tent-shaped lodge called a "Wig-wa-si-ga-mig" or—as the whites called it—a wigwam. The frame was left standing from year to year and hides and bark were used to enclose the shelter when in use.

During their stay, Johnny and Wa-me-gon-a-biew also had time to do a little trapping—mostly for muskrats—and speared spawning fish in the creek that ran close to camp. This experience was a first for Johnny and he really enjoyed it. Since the fish "ran" mostly at night, the boys used pine knot torches for illumination. Spears were made from forked saplings with barbs carved into the points so that the fish could not slip off when being taken from the stream. The light from the torch seemed to hypnotize the fish and if the boys were careful, they would not move until the spear hit them. No one explained to Johnny that light refraction in the water distorted the location of the fish farther out in the stream (they seemed farther away than they actually were) and once when he reached too far out he not only overshot his target but the surprisingly deep water drew him off balance—head-first into the icy creek. Of course, Wa-me-gon-a-biew had a few appropriate comments but never did explain the phenomenon to Johnny, hoping he would repeat the dunking—and he did. But before the night-time adventure was over, the white boy had the consolation of spearing the biggest fish—a long, deep-bodied northern pike that went at least 20 pounds.

With the completion of the sugar harvest, the families returned to Burntwood Camp. A few days later, as the evening meal was shared, Net-no-kwa looked across the campfire at the Smoker and in her soft voice spoke these words of appreciation, "Pot-wan-we-ninne, you have been good to me and my sons. When we were near starvation you took us home with you. We have been well fed during a hard and difficult winter. My boys came to your lodge thin and scrawny from hunger; now they are fat and each is at least an inch taller. Shaw-shaw-wa-be-na-se and Wa-me-gon-a-biew have learned much from your ex-ample—not only how to be a good hunter and trapper but something about what it means to be a brave. We can never repay you for your kindness. But we have accepted your hospitality long enough; the time has come for us to return to Grand Portage where we will join the first brigade of canoes going west."

The Smoker spoke, "It has been good having you and your sons in our lodge. If you must go, I will guide you back to the fort. But we will miss your gentle manner and Wa-me-gon-a-biew's teasing and little Falcon's quick smile."

The return journey was easy and uneventful. At the fort the Smoker and Net-no-kwa moved among the Indians and whites inquiring when the first canoes would be heading for Red River. Towards the close of the day, Pot-wan-we-ninne sought out Net-no-kwa, bringing with him another Muskegee Indian—a huge man nearly a head taller than himself.

"Net-no-kwa, look who I found, your relative, Wa-ge-mah-wub. Unless you had better fortune than I, it looks as though no canoes will be going your way until after the rendezvous. Meanwhile, Wa-ge-mah-wub and his family will be leading a party of about 30 to Isle Royal. He assures me you and the boys are welcome to go along—unless, of course, you would like to return to Burntwood."

Wa-ge-mah-wub added his own words of assurance, "You are indeed welcome, my cousin. There is plenty of room in our canoes for you and my young relatives. You will find much game there—and many sturgeon, and beaver and otter furs that will still be in prime."

Net-no-kwa seldom consulted the boys on important decisions. She felt that was her responsibility as an adult, but this time she turned to Johnny and Wa-me-gon-a-biew and asked, "What do you think, my sons?"

Johnny looked at Wa-me-gon-a-biew. Their eyes met and they both smiled. Then, reading each other's mind they spoke as one, "Let us go to the island!"

The next few days were extremely windy and even though the harbor was sheltered by two points and Mutton Island, the breakers rolled far up on the beach. But one morning the wind blew gently off the shore and word went forth that the expedition would leave just as soon as the canoes could be loaded. Johnny was a bit apprehensive about another trip on the open waters of Lake Superior and was quick to join others in bringing a food offering to the scraggly witch's tree which grew out of the rocky shore overlooking the lake where he prayed for a safe voyage. The journey was pleasantly uneventful and majestic Isle Royal soon loomed in the distance. It seemed to Johnny, however, that the island just didn't get any closer and he was one happy boy when he finally hopped out of the canoe and stretched his legs.

The final destination proved to be a lake within the island, and by the evening of the second day everyone was busy setting up camp. Net-no-kwa and her sons chose an open spot between two gigantic white pines, only a few steps from the water's edge. It had been quite a trip, and everyone had earned a full night's sleep.

The men of the tribe lost no time the next morning in laying their traplines. It would soon be summer and the animals would be shedding and growing their new coats of hair, making the pelts worthless until the next fall. Wa-ge-mah-wub's sons were grown up and on their own, and he took pride and delight in taking Johnny and Wa-me-gon-a-biew with him. He taught them his secret techniques of trapping and netting and even showed them how to mold lead balls for their muzzle loaders. The boys were cautioned to always try to retrieve the bullets from their fallen animals because they could be used again and again. Wa-ge-mah-wub told how he had once killed 20 moose and elk with only seven balls.

The boys used their own traps and were allowed to keep all they caught. Wa-ge-mah-wub also taught them the dead-fall technique where one end of a heavy log was propped up with pieces of sappling. The bait was then set in back of the props in such a way that the animal was likely to trip the supports, dropping the timber and hopefully breaking its back. Even such a huge animal as the black bear could be taken in this manner. Net-no-kwa applied her many years of experience to the care of the hides the boys brought home, keeping them in first class condition and at peak value. It wasn't long before scores of beaver, otter and other pelts were accumulated.

One day, Wa-ge-mah-wub pointed out a huge sturgeon making its way slowly up the stream than ran to Lake Superior. "Tomorrow," he said, "we will bring our sturgeon spears with us. These fish are important to us. Not only is their flesh good to eat—especially when smoked—but the cord from the back can be cooked to make glue."

The spear heads had been procured from the white traders and were specially made with hand-forged iron tines and barbs. Wooden spears, even those made of the hardest of woods, rarely penetrated the almost armor-like skin of these remnants of prehistoric days. In earlier times, Indians had made their sturgeon spears of the copper native to this area.

Spearing sturgeon was a waiting game, and since the huge fish seemed to avoid the banks of the stream, the fishermen took turns standing in the cold water.

Wa-ge-mah-wub was first to score. It was a magnificent specimen—easily 60 or 70 pounds—and the big man had his hands full beaching the huge fish. Wa-me-gon-a-biew missed his first opportunity; the spear actually seemed to glance off the sturgeon's back. But his second try on a 10 or 12 pounder was a success. Johnny had three opportunities that morning but either he wasn't strong enough or else the spear just glanced off the leathery hide. Wa-me-gon-a-biew knew how badly Johnny felt and for a change refrained from teasing him. That night the feast of first fruits was celebrated. Even though Wa-me-gon-a-biew had been kind enough not to rib Johnny for being "skunked"—the white boy couldn't resist observing at the end of the feast, as he looked his Indian brother straight in the eye, "Not bad for a minnow."

Wa-me-gon-a-biew let out a scream and was all over Johnny in an instant. Caught in the vice-like grip of his older brother's muscular legs around his very full middle, he admitted through tears of hysterical laughter—at Wa-me-gon-a-biew's prompting—that the sturgeon was the finest, the most beautiful, the best tasting sturgeon he had ever seen or eaten!

The next day, Wa-ge-mah-wub and the boys laid a net for sturgeon. It had been soaked overnight in a herb solution to take away human scent and attract the fish. The following morning they found one of the huge fish hopelessly entangled in its meshes. Wa-ge-mah-wub told the boys, "Until we have need for it, we will tie it up and keep it alive."

Johnny was surprised to see this accomplished by securing a tight loop around the smallest part of the fish, just in front of its stiff tail. The other end was tied to a tree, giving the sturgeon a fair amount of freedom. Over the next few days the process was repeated until a half dozen of the monsters were lined up in a row just off the bank of the stream, ready to be butchered as needed.

The island was well populated with woodland caribou and they proved fairly easy to hunt, just as long as they didn't smell the hunter. Johnny had never been privileged to shoot a big game animal, so one morning, with Wa-ge-mah-wub as guide, Wa-me-gon-a-biew as a "driver" and the white boy carrying the heavy muzzle loader, the three left camp on a "meat hunt". They went in the opposite direction from where they had been fishing and trapping because Wa-ge-mah-wub figured all the activity in that area had spooked the caribou into the timber between the camp and Lake Superior. He remembered a long ravine he had seen on the way in from the big lake that would possibly be narrow enough to be driven by two hunters. Johnny was placed "on stand" where he could get a fairly open shot at any running animal. He was cautioned to stand perfectly still and to keep a big Norway pine between himself and any oncoming caribou. His heart pounded with anticipation as he waited impatiently for Wa-me-gon-a-biew and Wa-ge-mah-wub to circle to the far end of the ravine and then work their way towards him with the wind. Countless times he raised the heavy weapon and tried to site down the long barrel at imaginary caribou. He had been told he had to lead a running animal, but he wasn't sure how far—realizing that distance would be as important a factor as speed. Then he began to worry.

"What if I miss?"

"Wa-me-gon-a-biew would never let me live it down if I missed so large a target."

"And if I do miss, I'll never get the gun reloaded before the caribou will be out of sight."

Then he heard it—the snap of a broken branch back up the ravine. Then another crack. . .and another. . .and another. . .getting close now . . .it had to be caribou!

Then he saw it—a huge bull, antlerless this time of year—moving at full trot. He brought the muzzle loader to his shoulder, but as he tried to draw a bead, he was aware the barrel was waving wildly. Then—miracle of miracles—the caribou stopped and looked back in the direction of the drivers. Johnny braced the barrel against the big tree behind which he had been hiding, took a fine bead on a spot in back of the front shoulder, and squeezed the trigger. The gun roared. The caribou leaped forward and charged out of sight before Johnny could even think of reloading. His heart sank.

"How could I have missed?" he wondered in disbelief.

"Maybe I didn't—maybe he's wounded." Johnny hoped.

Without reloading he ran to the spot where the caribou had stood—and there was a blood trail, spattered heavily on the ground and bushes. With shaking hands and fingers that seemed all thumbs, Johnny tried to reload: powder, patch and ball—or was it ball, powder and patch? Finally he got the order clear in his mind—he was right the first time he decided—and rammed it home.

"I should wait for Wa-me-gon-a-biew and Wa-ge-mah-wub," he thought, but then rationalized, "It won't hurt to go a little way."

The trail couldn't have been easier to follow if it had been painted with a brush. Johnny's heart was doing flip-flops as he ran along, nose to the ground. Then he saw the caribou—about two hundred yards from where he had shot—hung up on a windfall it had failed to clear, and deader than a door nail! He was still standing there admiring his trophy when he became aware of his partners trotting up. Wa-me-gon-a-biew grabbed Johnny in a bear hug that squeezed the breath right out of him. As the animal was butchered, Johnny recounted the details of his triumph, and the story got better as he went along. He never did mention that the caribou was standing still when he shot. In fact by the time they were back in camp, he told his mother the kill was at 100 paces and the animal was running at top speed with so many bushes and trees in the way that he only had a moment when the caribou was in the open for his single shot!

Wa-ge-mah-wub and Wa-me-gon-a-biew exchanged knowing glances, but neither had the heart to question the account.

The following evening, Net-no-kwa invited the whole tribe to share in the feast of Ostenetahgawin. Johnny had made her very proud.

No one was quite sure of the date, but the occasion was also used to mark Johnny's thirteenth birthday; he had become a teenager!

With the coming of summer, the animal pelts lost their prime, so the tribe prepared for its return journey to Grand Portage. The day they reached Lake Superior the wind was strong from the west, so they waited. The third day the wind went down with the sun. A full moon appeared over the lake and it was decided they would travel by night. When all the canoes were loaded, they proceeded out a little way from shore where Wa-ge-mah-wub called a halt. Reverently he raised up in his canoe, looked up at the night sky, and addressed the Great Spirit, "You who created each of us, your children, the trees on the hillside, the moon above and the lake on which we travel—surely has control over the wind and the waves. Give us quiet waters and a safe journey."

With that, he took a small amount of tobacco from his pouch and cast it on the surface of the lake. Someone is each of the canoes did the same. Then, as the Indians picked up their paddles and turned into the west, he sang a song of praise to the Great Spirit.

For Johnny, it was a strong reminder of his own religious upbringing, and as the procession continued on peaceful waters disturbed only by dancing moonbeams, he concluded, "Wa-ge-mah-wub prayed to the same God I was taught to believe in; he was just calling Him by his Indian name."

CHAPTER VII
THE
VOYAGEURS' TRAIL

Shortly after returning to Grand Portage, Johnny and Wa-me-gon-a-biew enjoyed their second Rendezvous of the Voyageurs. Each day leading up to that great event brought more and more "men of the north" down the portage trail behind the great fort, laden with their treasures of furs. And more and more heavily loaded Montreal canoes arrived by way of Lake Superior, powered by their singing crews and carrying trade goods from all over the world:

> glass beads from Italy,
> wine from France,
> rum from the West Indies, and
> cloth and hardware from England.

Hundreds of Indians also came on the scene from their winter camps, and soon the whole area was teeming with people and bustling with activity. A group of Ojibway from Rainy Lake brought more sad news for Net-no-kwa; her son-in-law had been killed in a drunken frolic by an older Indian. It had been an accident, but that made it no less tragic—leaving two little girls without a father. The news made Net-no-kwa all the more determined to depart for Rainy Lake just as soon as possible, but no one was interested in leaving before the end of the Rendezvous, and she knew better than to "go it alone" with her little family through an unmarked wilderness. She had no choice but to wait, impatiently, through the two weeks of fighting, dancing, drinking, wagering and good natured rivalry—all of which added to her unhappiness by serving as a reminder that it was just one year ago on this same occasion when she lost her beloved Tau-ga-we-ninne. Johnny and Wa-me-gon-a-biew, on the other hand, didn't want to miss a single day of the carnival-like celebration. Although too young to join in, there were no more enthusiastic spectators.

Early in the Rendezvous, Net-no-kwa had traded the furs the boys had accumulated on Isle Royal for the things they would need on their trip west—including ornaments and trinkets she wouldn't mind keeping for herself but which could serve as trade goods in an emergency. She also arranged for a canoe to be made ready for them at Fort Charlotte, up on the Pigeon River. So when the Rendezvous was over and the first group of Indians announced they were ready to leave and would be passing through Rainy Lake, Net-no-kwa was all packed and ready to go. With wisdom accumulated over the years, she traveled light, knowing what a struggle it could be for her and the boys on the rough portages—and there would be so many of them.

The Voyageurs' highway was indeed a busy thoroughfare in the days following the Rendezvous. Between five and six hundred of the flamboyant French Canadians traveled the waterways leading to Rainy Lake along with almost as many Indians. A few parties of voyageurs branched off to the north or south along the way at such places as Vermillion River, but the vast majority would follow the route all the way to Lake of the Woods. Here, some would go north or south, but again, the majority would travel on—to Lake Winnepeg, the Red River and points north—a relatively few paddling and portaging all the way to Lake Athabasca.

For Johnny, it was the most beautiful country he had ever seen. Of course the first couple of days' journey as far as Moose Lake was a repeat of the previous summer when Kewatin was still living and the family had traveled that far before giving up out of concern for the boy's health. Little did Johnny realize that in his lifetime he would travel these waterways and portages between Lake Superior and the Lake of the Woods a dozen times and more and would come to know them as well as any voyageur.

The first night out of Fort Charlotte was spent on a meadow-like campsite along the Pigeon River. The open area was shared by scores of Indians and voyageurs—it was chosen because it was not only about the right distance for the first days work, but was also an easy place to pitch camp. The group of Indians with whom Net-no-kwa and her sons were traveling were from a tribe of Ojibway which lived on One Sided Lake (Caliper Lake) just east of Sabaskong Bay of Lake of the Woods. They were a friendly and considerate lot who not only made the Ottawa family feel welcome but even helped carry their possessions on the longer portages. Johnny, at 13, was still very much a boy, and even though he tried to carry his share, he was no match for his 16-year-old brother who had noticeably begun to put on muscle and weight. Always the teaser, Wa-me-gon-a-biew enjoyed showing off his newly found strength and was forever throwing choice comments over his shoulder at his struggling white brother such as, "If it's too much for you, *little* Falcon, wait here and I'll come back and carry both you and your baggage."

Or, "If you can't keep up your end of the canoe, climb in and I'll carry you and the canoe, too!"

Johnny had one answer, "Just you wait—some day I'll be bigger than you and I won't forget your big talk!"

But in his heart, he wasn't sure he would ever catch up with the fast-growing Wa-me-gon-a-biew.

The second day out of Fort Charlotte took the travelers over several portages, but at Great Stone and Caribou the water was low enough so they could wade their canoe rather than unload and carry everything overland. Portaging was hard work and there was always the temptation for the daring voyageurs to shoot even the more dangerous rapids. Many a foolhardy Frenchman paid with his life trying to avoid carrying the heavy loads over the rough or muddy terrain. As many as a score or more of wooden crosses stood in grim testimony along the more difficult rapids, a silent but effective reminder that the portage in those places was well worth the effort.

Between Caribou and Goose Portages the river wound through lowlands and extensive swamps; then came the clear, green waters of South Fowl Lake, and Pigeon River was behind them. Next, after going through a short stream lined with rushes, came North Fowl Lake and Moose Portage, and then Moose Lake itself. The Indians camped that night on the very place which Net-no-kwa, O-gay-bow, Wa-me-gon-a-biew, Kewatin and Johnny had called home the previous year. As Johnny lay down to sleep that night, his mind was filled with memories of Kewatin, and he wept quietly, stifling his sobs in his blanket.

With dawn came a pleasant ride across the clear waters of Moose Lake. Johnny watched fish scurry out of the way of the canoe whenever they entered shallow water and he reminded Wa-me-gon-a-biew of their good luck the previous year netting lake trout, whitefish, walleyes and northerns.

Great Cherry Portage was next and it proved to be especially long and difficult. The hardships of the trail were multiplied because they

had to retrace their steps several times to bring all of the family possessions plus the canoe itself to the other side. By the time all this was accomplished, Johnny wasn't sure he wanted to be a voyageur after all.

Upper and Lower Lily Lakes—with short second Cherry Portage in-
between—were well populated with broods of half-grown ducks. Excited hens flopped just ahead of the canoes, trying to look crippled and
thereby lure the invaders away from their young ones—which meanwhile scurried for cover into the vegetation closer to shore.

The third Cherry Portage brought the travelers to beautiful Mountain
Lake, and after a day of hard work on the portages and with the realization that the next day would bring more of the same, the tribe decided
to make camp even though it was scarcely past mid afternoon. Johnny
and Wa-me-gon-a-biew used the free time to troll for fish for supper and
managed to pick up a couple of nice northerns on their handline.

Watab Portage was the first order of business the next day, followed
by an interesting "detroit" or narrow passage to Rove Lake. Then came
the very rough "new" Long Portage. Even the voyageurs stopped to rest
and enjoy their clay pipes; it was a quiet day and the smoke hung heavy
along the trail. On the other end of the portage lay six-mile-long Rose
Lake. The Ojibway called it "Small Fish Lake", because about all that
was in it was suckers. The French speaking voyageurs described it with
the word "roseau", meaning muddy, but the English apparently thought
they were saying "rose", and that name stuck. The long portage had
been a struggle and it was decided to go no farther that day.

When travel was resumed the following morning, Rat Portage and
Rat Lake were next, but the latter was more of a puddle than a lake.
The name, of course, came from all the muskrats which lived in the
area. Net-no-kwa warned the boys, "People say these waters have a
mysterious wendigo (evil spirit) who lives in the muddy depths and who
is so powerful it can suck a canoe right out of sight! We must paddle
hard and not let up."

She was serious. The boys exchanged knowing glaces and Johnny
suppressed a snicker, but after crossing the lake they agreed they could
feel something pulling on their canoe, trying to hold it back.

South Lake Portage led to South Lake, or, Height of Land Lake, as
the Indians called it. The portage that followed—and the place where
they camped that night—truly was high ground and marked the con-
tinental divide for that area. Waters running south and east from here
flow to the Atlantic Ocean via Lake Superior and the St. Lawrence
watershed. Waters running north or west end up in Hudson Bay via

The voyageurs could carry unbelievably heavy loads.

Rainy Lake, Rainy River, Lake of the Woods and the water chain leading north from there.

Several crews of voyageurs shared the campsite with the Indians that night and entertained them with their initiation of a couple of "pork eaters" converting to "hommes du nord" (men of the north). The ceremony was simple—several of the men spattered the initiates with swamp water by shaking wet cedar boughs in their faces. They were made to promise they would never let any other greenhorns pass this way without similar treatment, and then were expected to treat the rest of the crew with high wine. The climax was the firing of twelve well-spaced shots from muzzleloaders. The alcohol eventually took effect and noisy dancing and general merriment followed. The men took turns beating time on kettles or whatever else was handy and noisy while others sang and danced jigs or rounds, circling with arms locked or placed on each others' shoulders. Johnny marveled how they had so much energy left after paddling and portaging all day.

The morning brought them to North Lake with its clear, turquois-colored waters. A forest fire had ravaged the high hills on the east side of the lake, leaving only black trunks and stumps where once stood a green forest. Johnny said something about it being "too bad", but Net-no-kwa remarked, "Good dryberry (blueberry) picking in a few years and much food for birds and animals next year. Food for birds and animals means food for the Indian."

Short Portage was next, leading them to Gunflint Lake, appropriately named as a source of flint for firemaking and for flintlock guns. The lake itself was most beautiful, only one or two miles wide but seven miles long. Although the day was a windy one, the travelers were quite sheltered. Since some difficult terrain lay ahead, it was decided this would be a good place to make camp. Several hours of daylight remained and the boys joined others in hunting partridges for supper. They brought back so many, Net-no-kwa used a shortcut method in cleaning them. She stood on their wings and gave both feet a quick pull. The bare breast was thus ripped from the rest of the carcass and broiled over the evening fire—good eating!

The shallow waters of midsummer made the next twelve miles most difficult; it was the Granite River chain of small lakes and short portages. The larger canoes of the voyageurs really had problems, but the Indians with their smaller and lighter crafts made it all the way in one day. Johnny was surprised to find an Indian operated birchbark canoe "factory" at the mouth of the Granite River, where it entered by Lake

Saganaga. Voyageurs and natives alike had trouble with their fragile crafts on these long journeys. They could be patched just so many times before their bark was worn thin or ruptured in just too many places. The village was strategically located for a good market.

Although their canoe had taken a beating because of the shallow water, Net-no-kwa felt certain it would make it to Rainy Lake, but others in the party were not so sure about their vessels and their negotiations resulted in a late start the next morning. Saganaga was huge, and even though there were many islands of pine and rock for shelter, good weather was necessary to assure a safe crossing. By afternoon, a brisk breeze had grown into a strong wind and it was decided to hold up on Voyageurs Island. Rather than go through all the work of unloading and reloading the canoes, and since the vessels were too fragile to pull up on shore when loaded, they were moored off the leeward side of the island and held in place by light cedar poles—with one end across the gunwale and the other anchored to shore. Around the family campfire that night, Net-no-kwa told how not too many years earlier the Dakota-Sioux had made a surprise attack on an Ojibway village on this lake, completely destroying it and killing almost everyone.

The wind went down during the night and calm waters made easy paddling across the remainder of Saganaga. The party then entered an interesting chain of lakes and portages on the south side of huge Hunters Island, which was bordered by a similar string of small lakes and narrow waterways on its north side.

Cypress Lake, which came next, was among the more beautiful—four miles long but so narrow it seemed like a river. They then crossed Little Knife Portage and Little Knife Lake, from which they followed a narrow, rock-bound passageway to Knife Lake itself. Then, Big Knife Portage led to Birch Lake ("Well named," Johnny thought) and then Prairie Portage skirted a series of cascades and waterfalls to Basswood.

Around the campfire that night, Net-no-kwa asked the boys, "Remember what I told you about the Dakota-Sioux attacking a village of Ojibway back on Saganaga? Well, the same thing happened here."

"There aren't any Sioux around here now, are there?" Johnny asked a bit apprehensively.

"No possibility," Net-no-kwa assured, "Far too many voyageurs and Ojibway here now. Besides, the Dakota-Sioux have been driven out of the woodlands and back to the plains a long way west of here. But I do worry a little about the Red River area where we will end up. That is not far from Dakota country.

"But it is said there will be many Assinneboines where we are going. Their name means 'Sioux of the rocks'. Why aren't we concerned about them?" Wa-me-gon-a-biew asked.

"That is a long story," the mother replied, "They were driven into the northlands by their cousins the Winnebagos many moons ago. The Ojibway, Cree and Ottawa received them as friends because of their common enemy—the Dakotas—so they have always considered the Algonquin Tribes as allies."

"Algonquin tribes?" Johnny asked, "Who are they?"

"We are Algonquins," Net-no-kwa explained, "But besides the Ottawa there are the Ojibway, the Cree, the Shawnee, the Menominees, the Fox, the Potawatomi and others. All of them are Algonquins."

"Oh," Johnny responded.

"The Sioux nation," Net-no-kwa went on, "includes an even larger group of related tribes. Besides the Dakotas, they are the Winnebagos, the Assinneboines, the Iowas, the Mandans, the Crows, the Hidatsas and more. And to make it even more confusing, there are seven councils of Dakotas."

Johnny looked across the fire at his brother and teased, "Since I am a white I can choose whatever kind of Indian I want to be—I think I will choose to be a—Dakota-Sioux and scalp you! But not until I tie you to a tree and build a big fire close by!"

"Oh, now you have really got me scared!" Wa-me-gon-a-biew snorted.

"Strange you should say that Shaw-shaw-wa-be-na-se," Net-no-kwa interjected, "We sometimes call the Sioux "roasters". Some say it is because that is the way they torture their victims".

Both boys gulped, and that was the end of the conversation for the night.

After leaving Basswood, the party entered a narrow channel between the cliffs and rocky islands of Crooked Lake. At one point, Net-no-kwa stopped paddling and pointed to a crack in the rock cliff about 30 or 40 feet above the water. The weathered shafts of several arrows were visible. She explained, "Those arrows were shot there by the Sioux as a warning to the Ojibway."

"Wow!" Johnny said, "They were good shots."

Near the arrows, on a flat surface of the rock wall, were painted the figures of moose, horned men and a heron. Johnny wondered what artist put them there.

At the end of the lake, they came to beautiful Curtain Falls, which dropped about 20 feet over a 100 foot expanse. After crossing Bottle Portage they reached famous Lac la Croix and made camp. While visiting with their fellow travelers, they were told about another old Indian route which led from this lake to Lake Superior. It was called the "Kaministiquia route", because much of the time it followed the river by that name. Little did anyone in that day suspect this more northernly way would eventually become the chief Canadian route to the west. After 1800, when it was established that much of the Grand Portage route, as well as Grand Portage itself, was on American soil, the Canadians would be thankful to have this alternate passage available so that they could avoid paying duty.

The next day, as they crossed Lac la Croix, they saw more paintings on the granite cliffs. While entering Loon Lake, Net-no-kwa told her sons, "Remind me to tell you a story tonight about this lake. I will give you a clue. . .The Ojibway call it Un-de-go-sa, or "Maneaters Lake!"

That night, the party made camp on Sandpoint Lake, shortly after passing the mouth of the Vermillion River, where several canoes of voyageurs were seen turning south. After the evening meal had been completed, Johnny prodded Net-no-kwa, "Remember your promise, my Mother; what is the story of Maneaters Lake?"

"It is not a pretty tale," she began. "Many moons ago at the great Ojibway village on Madeline Island off the south shore of Lake Superior, at a place the French call La Pointe, there developed a cult of medicine men who did not walk with the Great Spirit. They were, instead, influenced by an evil Wendigo. Somehow they became obsessed with the thought that it would strengthen them in mind and body if they ate the flesh of the dead. They must have thought the abilities of the people they ate somehow were transferred to their bodies and minds. The custom spread and soon people weren't dying fast enough of natural causes so they would kill those who opposed them to satisfy their evil appetites. Finally there was nothing else the village people could do but flee for their lives, leaving the cannibals to themselves. It is thought that some from this village found their way to Maneaters Lake, because one winter when everyone was starving, these people turned to eating their own dead. When the other Indians learned about these degenerates, they would have nothing to do with them."

"There aren't any people like that left around here now, are there?" Johnny asked with his usual anxiety.

"Oh, my no." Net-no-kwa replied, "Yet their descendents even now must be somewhere trying to forget the evil deeds of their forefathers."

"What do you think, now, my little brother?" Wa-me-gon-a-biew teased, "I suppose instead of growing up to be a Dakota-Sioux you would prefer to join an Ojibway maneating tribe and have the revenge you're always boasting of by killing me and then roasting me over your campfire."

"Ugh!" Johnny blurted out, and then added after considerable pause, "You'd be too tough, and stringy, and sour—mostly sour!"

Neither boy slept very well that night.

Namakan Lake came next, then Bare Portage, and finally, Rainy Lake itself. Win-et-ka was living in a huge Ojibway village at the other end of the lake, near the Northwest trading post where Rainy River begins its journey to Lake of the Woods. Once there, finding her was no problem. After mother and daughter had a tearful reunion, Net-no-kwa turned to her two little granddaughters who had been watching the whole performance with eyes as big as saucers, and embraced them with that special kind of love only a grandparent can give. Meanwhile, Win-et-ka walked over to where Wa-ma-gon-a-biew and Johnny were standing and proceeded to embarrass her half-brother by "oohing and aahing" over how much he had grown and how handsome he had become. Then, with the grace of her mother, she turned to Johnny and put him at ease by saying, "You are welcome here, my brother, I know we will become good friends."

At this point, a tall brave approached the group and Win-et-ka turned to her mother and said with a broad smile, "There is some good news I have not told you, here comes Maji-go-bo, my new husband! He has taken me as his second wife."

For Net-no-kwa, good news was long overdue, and she was literally overcome with joy. Not only was she happy for her daughter and the girls, but now she wouldn't have to worry about taking them along to the Red River. She feared Wa-me-gon-a-biew and her little Falcon would be unable to support so many, especially should they be unable to find Tau-ga-we-ninne's family.

Maji-go-bo made his new relatives welcome and that same day helped them begin the construction of a new lodge next to his own. Even though Net-no-kwa had found her daughter in good hands, she decided she and the boys would stay on for awhile, perhaps even until next spring. The trip to the Red River would wait. It was more important that she spend some time with her daughter and get re-acquainted with her grandchildren. It would probably be a long time before they would pass that way again.

CHAPTER VIII
RAINY LAKE

In the years to come, Johnny would have many pleasant memories associated with the months the family would spend at Rainy Lake, and over those years he would return again and again to visit the village. Among the more interesting of those memories would be his exposure to several new facets of Ojibway religion and tradition.

Shortly after Net-no-kwa and the boys arrived at the village, the very secret and mysterious Midewinin ceremony was held. The ever-curious Johnny heard about the preparations and had many questions for his new brother-in-law, beginning with "What is the purpose of the ceremony? Is it something a person belongs to?"

"Whoa, Little Falcon—one question at a time." Maji-go-bo replied. "Yes, it is a secret society people belong to, but because it is secret there isn't a great deal I am permitted to tell you. However, it is common knowledge among all Indians that its purpose is to help its members stay in good health, heal them when they are sick, and make it possible for them to enjoy long life."

"Are you a member, Maji-go-bo?"

"Yes, I was initiated several years ago."

"Can anybody join?" Johnny asked.

"I guess so, but you must ask to be admitted. One becomes eligible to apply if he is healed by a member of the society or if he has a vision or a dream in which the Great Spirit makes it clear that he should seek membership."

"Is the chief the leader?" was the next question.

"No, the society is run by the medicine men; they are called 'Shamans'. You will be allowed to witness the ceremonies and the

Shamans will be the ones who direct the proceedings."

At this point Maji-go-bo stopped talking, so Johnny prodded him with, "Tell me more."

"There really isn't much more I am allowed to tell you, except, maybe, that there are "degrees" of accomplishment or honors one may attain—four of them in all—but I cannot tell you anything more about them. I understand other lodges have eight degrees and it is said degrees are sometimes taught beyond the customary four or eight, but those often teach black magic. Some of these evil Shamans who teach additional degrees are called "Bear Walkers" because they are said to go about at night disguised in a bear skin taking vengeance on their enemies."

Johnny's curiosity was really piqued by this time, but he knew it would be improper to pursue the inquiry further.

On the first day of the ceremony Maji-go-bo took Wa-me-gon-a-biew and Johnny with him to witness the big event. As they drew near the far side of the village, Johnny was surprised to see an enormous lodge, about 200 feet long, approximately 30 feet wide, and maybe 10 feet high. It was constructed in the same manner as the lodges the Indians lived in, with the larger end of small trees set into the ground and the tops bent over and lashed together at the middle. But just the framework was there, there was no hide or bark covering and the spectators could see all that went on inside. However, only the members or those about to join were admitted into the enclosure.

As the participants arrived, some carried drums of skin stretched over hollow sections of logs or across a wooden circular frame, others carried rattles. Many had pipes, and still others carried what looked like scrolls of birchbark. "What do you suppose those birchbark rolls are for?" Johnny asked his brother.

"I don't know but I understand there are pictures and symbols written on them that have some magical meaning," Wa-me-gon-a-biew replied.

The initiates stood in a separate group as they arrived, but before they were allowed to enter the big lodge they had to first take a steam bath in a small hut close to the lake as sort of a purification ceremony. Water was splashed on very hot rocks and the people stayed inside as long as they could stand the steam. When they could take no more they would dash to the water's edge and dive in.

Noticing that some were very young, Johnny asked Wa-me-gon-a-biew, "Why don't you belong to the lodge?"

"Midewinin practices were not common where we used to live," he replied.

The purging completed, the initiates approached the enclosure and the ceremony commenced. Those who were already members were the first to enter the lodge—following the medicine men, and led by the chief Shaman. Each initiate brought a dead dog which he lay in front of the entrance and which he had to step over as he entered the lodge. The dogs would later be roasted and eaten during the ceremony. As a part of the ritual, present lodge members stood around the doorway and tried to dissuade the new members from entering. However, each initiate looked neither to the right nor to the left but kept his eyes straight ahead on the medicine pole which had been erected as the focal point in the enclosure. The new members also carried gifts for the Shamans; the higher the degree they were seeking, the more valuable the gift. The hundred or more occupants of the lodge followed the leadership of the Shamans—dancing, singing, shaking their rattles, beating their drums and repeating secret words and phrases as they paraded around the inside of the enclosure. After more than an hour of these preliminary activities, everyone sat down in their previously assigned positions. Later in the day the new members were initiated.

For the boys, the most intriguing part of the ceremony was when the Shamans pretended to shoot snail and clam shells into the bodies of the new members. Each pretended to be struck down as though dead but then with the encouragement of the medicine men made believe they were coughing up the shells into their hands. These shells were supposed to have great magical and protective powers and were placed in their medicine pouches for safe keeping.

At first enthralled, the boys watched spellbound, but when the activity became repetitious and—to them meaningless— they gradually lost interest. When the second day proved to be very much like the first, the boys decided not to return for the last two days of the ceremony. However, they did talk about how it would be nice to belong to the society someday. In fact, Johnny was a bit hurt and disappointed when Maji-go-bo said he wasn't sure a white Indian could be admitted. He told him, "That would be up to the Shamans."

A few days after the ceremony, one of the Shamans visited Net-no-kwa and blessed her new lodge, driving out the evil spirits (windigoes) and assuring protection against their return. As a symbol of his blessing, he erected a 20 foot cedar pole in front of the lodge at the top of which was a fairly good carving of his personal totem, a beaver. Of course Net-no-kwa was obligated to present the medicine man with a gift in appreciation for his services. After some brief negotiations, he settled for one of the silver ornaments off her dress.

With his mind on religion, Johnny thought about another ceremony he had heard of for older boys, through which they were accepted as men in the eyes of the tribe. Once again he sought out Maji-go-bo—his new hero and source of all wisdom.

"Of course you can go through the initiation," the brother-in-law assured him, "White boys have to grow up to become men, too."

Johnny was so delighted he took off at once in search of Wa-me-gon-a-biew to tell him the good news. By the time he found his brother, a dozen questions were in his mind, he wished he had asked Maji-go-bo, but he poured them out to Wa-me-gon-a-biew instead, one after the other in rapid fire order, and the older boy answered as best he could.

"Of course I've been through the ceremony, just before we found you."

"You know I have a medicine pouch."

"You know I cannot tell you what's in it. And don't you ever try to find out or terrible things will happen to you."

"Yes, you go away into the bush all by yourself—for ten days—and you don't eat a thing all that time and you don't dare to talk to anyone, that is, if you happen to see somebody out there."

"What do you mean, 'Is that all there is to it?' It's really difficult! Just wait 'til *you* try it."

"Yes, there is one thing more. While you are fasting you must pray every day to the Great Spirit that he will give you a vision or a least a dream that will show you your guardian spirit. It could be an animal, a bird, a fish or even a reptile."

"Sure I had a dream. But you know I cannot tell you about my guardian spirit. That will be a secret all my life. But I guess I can tell you that it is a bird. I carry one of its feathers in my medicine pouch."

"Wow," Johnny said (half to himself and obviously in awe), "When can I become a brave?"

For once in his life, Wa-me-gon-a-biew resisted a sarcastic response, "Maybe next year. You will be 14 in the spring. That is how old I was. But it would help if your voice would change."

For weeks after that Johnny made a conscious effort of talking in as low a voice as possible!

Summer turned to fall and Johnny had his first try at duck hunting with a muzzleloader. In previous years he had been lucky enough to get a few ducks with his wooden, blunt-headed arrows—and luck is the right word! He also had joined in the late summer chases of molting ducks and geese when the birds lost their wing feathers and could not fly for a couple of weeks, making them and their half-grown young ones relatively easy prey. It may not sound very sportsmanlike, but when it is a matter of getting enough food to eat, that really isn't very important.

One evening in mid-October, just at sunset, bluebills and mallards began to pour into Rainy Lake—just clearing the tops of the trees as they swooped down in search of food and rest after a long flight from the fast-freezing lakes farther north. After supper that night, Maji-go-bo walked over to Net-no-kwa's campfire and hunkered down by the boys. Following a few random remarks he looked first at Wa-me-gon-a-biew and then at Johnny and asked, "How about hunting some ducks tomorrow?"

"Sure, why not?" the boys responded with enthusiasm.

Johnny didn't sleep much that night.

Before dawn the three hunters were in their canoe and heading upshore towards a big rice bed. Pulling in just short of the bay, Maji-go-bo whispered final instructions to the boys: "Wa-me-gon-a-biew, you sneak around to the far side. I'll follow you and stop at the end of the bay. Little Falcon, you wait until you think we've had plenty of time to get into position around the rice bed and then sneak in about half way down the bay. Make your shot count. When you get in range, don't shoot until the ducks bunch up so you have a chance to get three or four in one shot. The pattern of your shot should cover about two bird lengths. If someone else shoots and the birds get up, just stay put until they come back and then sneak on them."

The boys nodded their understanding. Then Maji-go-bo and Wa-me-gon-a-biew were off, moving silently through the thick brush and staying well back from the water so that the ducks would not hear them. Johnny waited. . .and waited. . .and waited. He could hear the mallards, lots of mallards, quacking as they awakened and began feeding. Then he made his sneak. The soft light of morning was just enough so he could make his way without snapping twigs or stumbling over logs. When he was close enough so he could see patches of water and rice through the brush he dropped to his knees and began to crawl; he could hear ducks clucking and quacking directly ahead. Whoom! Wa-me-gon-a-biew's muzzle loader went off across the bay. Through the branches he could see the sky fill with ducks. His heart sank. Then another shot; he knew Wa-me-gon-a-biew had picked off a cripple. Johnny stayed hidden as he had been told and the hungry mallards continued to circle and finally began dropping back in. About a dozen mallards swung by, wings set, the emerald green of the drakes' heads glistening in the first rays of the rising sun. He heard them splash down. With his heart beating like a trip-hammer, he crawled the last 25 or so yards down to the shore on his stomach. Carefully he raised up until he could peek through the cattails. There they were, easily in range—but scattered all over throughout the patches of rice. He'd have to wait.

"But what if Wa-me-gon-a-biew or Maji-go-bo shoot first?" Johnny wondered to himself.

Two enormous green heads were swimming towards each other. . he could get them both. . .maybe he should shoot. . .no one would ever know if he hadn't waited for more ducks to come together. . .he just had to shoot something. . .what if he got skunked?. . .but more ducks were coming together now, bunching just right!. . .the squeeze of the trigger. . .Whoom!

When the smoke cleared, the patch of rice was full of flapping wings and kicking feet—five mallards in one shot! The air was once again filled with ducks, but Johnny had his mind on re-loading just as fast as he could in case there were cripples—but no problem, they were all his.

This time the ducks left the bay, but as the day wore on they returned in twos and threes and small flocks. Johnny had more shooting and potted more mallards, but three was the most he hit at any one time with his pattern of pellets—and one of those was a cripple at that but he managed to re-load in time to nail it before it swam out of range.

That evening when it was his turn to rest from paddling on the way back to the lodge, Johnny picked up his mallards one at a time and admired their heft and their beautiful plumage. He was particularly fascinated by one of the ducks Wa-me-gon-a-biew had shot. It was one of the most beautiful birds Johnny had ever seen—brillantly colored. Maji-go-bo identified it as a "Skah-rud" or wood duck. Before turning the birds over to Net-no-kwa and Win-et-ka for cleaning, he plucked the drakes' curly tails and put them away among his treasurers.

Another memory Johnny would long associate with Rainy Lake was his introduction to sled dogs for winter travel. The dogs belonged to his brother-in-law. They were big, long legged, long haired, sharp eared, and only a few generations removed from their wolf ancestors. As a boy, Maji-go-bo had captured two little timber wolf cubs. He raised them with his own dogs—themselves actually of wolf origin but countless generations removed. Eventually he bred the wolves with his dogs in the hope of developing a large strain with more speed, strength and stamina. He chose the four biggest and best of the offspring for his team and drove them in tandem before his long, hardwood toboggan, which he called his "No-bug-i-da-van". The wolf dogs were inclined to be less friendly and more prone to fight than the Indian dogs, but their performance made these problems well worth putting up with. Maji-go-bo allowed Johnny and Wa-me-gon-a-biew to drive his other dogs occasionally and the boys really loved it.

The Rainy Lake village was very large and the men had to branch out long distances in all directions to find enough game to hunt and trap. Maji-go-bo's area, which he had inherited from his father before him, was two days' journey up the shore in a north-easterly direction. Here he had a spike camp out of which he ran his trap lines. Johnny and Wa-me-gon-a-biew enjoyed trapping with Maji-go-bo; they thought it was "just great" having a brother-in-law so young who liked a good time as much as they. It was a mild winter, making the out-of-doors not only bearable but enjoyable. But it was not always so. Maji-go-bo told the boys, "Some winters the cold is so severe we cannot go on the trap lines for days at a time."

"We know," Johnny assured him, "Last winter we almost froze to death when we fell in a river."

"Some years," Maji-go-bo went on, "the snow is so deep and powdery you cannot travel in the bush even with snowshoes, and it lays so heavy on the ice that water comes up through the cracks and forms slush and that makes it impossible to travel on the lake as well."

The hunting and trapping were very good that winter, but Maji-go-bo told the boys it was not always so productive. "Some winters game is scarce. It seems to go in cycles. Disease, over-hunting, too much snow, lack of food—all make a difference. When I was a boy we went through several years when there was no big game and we lived on rabbits and fish during the winter months."

"Is it ever so bad the village goes hungry?" Johnny asked, thinking of their own dire condition the previous winter at Grand Portage before Pot-wan-we-ninne had come to their rescue.

"Unfortunately, the answer to your question is 'yes'. We have had many difficult winters in my lifetime. Besides, there are so many mouths to feed in our village."

"Does it ever get so bad people starve?" asked the ever curious Johnny.

"Not exactly," was the reply, "But many times there has been so little food people became weak and their bodies could not resist diseases and then they died from all kinds of sickness."

"I'm sure glad this isn't one of those years." Johnny said, half to himself.

Later that winter Johnny had a particularly exciting encounter with a moose. As the hunters were leaving the village for the spike camp, the women folk advised Maji-go-bo that the meat supply was getting low and urged that they try to bring back a caribou or moose. They were about half way to camp when they spotted three moose crossing from the mainland to one of the larger islands. The animals entered the woods at the tip of a long point and disappeared.

Maji-go-bo directed, "They are working into the wind. If you both hurry ahead to the base of the point you can cut them off. They will smell you and turn back, perhaps attempting to cross to the mainland where they came from. I will tie the dogs here, on shore, and should reach the point before the moose come out or at least be in range when they do."

The boys were off at a trot. Neither was wearing snowshoes because the strong winds of recent days had left the lake with only a light cover. The base of the point where it joined the main island was surprisingly narrow and the absence of tracks assured the boys they had the moose cut off. Looking back, the could see Maji-go-bo had nearly reached the tip of the point, so Wa-me-gon-a-biew suggested, "Let's spread out so that they won't get around us and then drive towards Maji-go-bo."

"Good," Johnny agreed.

The boys soon wished they had their snowshoes because the woods were filled with the soft snow blown off the lake. In places it reached Johnny's waist and the going was very slow. He couldn't lift his legs over the drifts and could only push his way into the powder. A short way in the point widened and the boys could no longer see each other. Then Johnny heard the animals crashing through the brush directly in front of him; they obviously did not like what they had smelled. Seconds later he heard Wa-me-gon-a-biew's muzzle loader discharge; the moose had tried to circle around Johnny and ran smack into the young Indian. But a running animal is not an easy target, even one as huge as a moose, and Wa-me-gon-a-biew missed. Now Johnny heard the crashing again, and coming closer. He was standing in a small clearing. Suddenly—right in front of him—the willows and sapplings began waving wildly and then parted as a big bull came charging through the drifts—the deep snow no challenge to its long legs. Johnny would never know whether the animal didn't see him or charged him intentionally. The monster was only a few yards away when he instinctively raised the heavy gun and shot. Johnny tried to lunge out of the way but couldn't run in the snow. Yet, the couple of steps he managed to take probably saved his life, because the moose collapsed in a pile right where he had stood—even brushing his leg as it went down!

In panic, Johnny dropped the rifle in the deep snow. Not sure the moose was really dead, he screamed, "Wa-me-gon-a-biew!" at the top of his voice. He had no need to fear, however, his ball had hit the moose in the neck, dead center, entering the spinal column. When Wa-me-gon-a-biew came up, puffing from exertion, he found his younger brother so shaken he was actually speechless for a change. But by the time Maji-go-bo arrived on the scene, Johnny had regained his speech (and his rifle) and never did stop talking all the while they were butchering the moose—cutting it into quarters so that it could be dragged out to the lake's edge and picked up by the dogsled.

As they were packing the meat on the toboggan, Maji-go-bo observed, "You are fortunate it is late winter and the bull had lost his antlers, or it is likely that instead of just brushing against you the wide antlers would have killed you or hurt you badly."

Johnny thought about that and even stopped jabbering for awhile.

A moose also played a role in another memorable experience for Johnny. It happened the next spring, shortly before the family left Rainy Lake.

Once the snow melted, Johnny began begging his mother to let him go through the manhood initiation ritual of fasting and praying by himself in the woods.

"I'm old enough; I'm soon fourteen. My voice is changing," he argued. And indeed it was—but it seemed at times to be going higher instead of lower!

"I am already taller than you, my mother," he added, and then went on, "If I don't do it now, we will soon be leaving for the west and who knows how long it will be until we are in one place long enough."

"Besides," he said, "Maji-go-bo can advise me; he won't be around to tell me what to do after we leave Rainy Lake."

"Huh," Wa-me-gon-a-biew snorted, "*I'll* be around to advise you; I've been through it all. There's nothing Maji-go-bo can tell you I don't know! Besides, the way your voice sounds I'm not so sure but what you're turning into a squaw!"

That did it. Tears began trickling down his cheeks and Johnny turned away so no one would see. But Net-no-kwa took notice and her heart was touched. "I will speak with Maji-go-bo tomorrow," she promised.

Johnny turned and unashamedly gave his mother a boyish hug.

True to her word, Net-no-kwa made the arrangements and a few days hence Maji-go-bo huddled with his new protege. He explained the rules of the game to Johnny. First he must blacken his face with charcoal, and then spend 10 days alone in the bush without eating or speaking to anyone he might chance to see. "And you must pray each day," he added, "petitioning the Great Spirit to show you your guardian spirit through a vision or a dream."

"This is a good time to ask me any other questions you would ask your father if he were here, about Indian ways or about growing into being a brave."

Never short on words, Johnny responded with a barrage of questions as though he might never again have the opportunity to ask an adult about anything. Only bedtime and complete weariness on Johnny's part saved Maji-go-bo from the marathon of inquiries.

After a day of stuffing himself with food almost to the point of becoming ill, Johnny took to the woods. The first three days were uneventful—but miserable. Johnny was tempted to eat even the buds on the trees, but he held firm to his commitment. By the third day, water seemed to satisfy his hunger pangs. He slept as much as he could, thus helping the time to pass and at the same time conserving his strength. The nights were the toughest. Johnny had never heard so many night sounds. He didn't mind the loons on the far off lake or the owls up in the tree tops, but raccoons, deer and other night creatures made suspicious noises as they moved through the dry leaves still on the ground from the previous autumn. At night a boy's imagination works overtime and he thought every raccoon was a skunk and every deer a lynx.

On the sixth morning, Johnny walked down to a stream for a drink of water, but found someone there before him—a cow moose and her twin calves. They had not noticed his approach so he clapped his hands and shouted expecting the clumsy calves to fall over each other trying to escape. To his surprise all three just stared at him. When the mother located the source of the disturbance she shook her big head and pawed the shallow water where she stood, throwing mud and rocks into the brush behind her. That was enough for Johnny and he took off into the woods, but he could hear the monstrous animal in pursuit! He knew he couldn't outrun her so he stopped behind a substantial clump of birch trees. Mother moose had no hesitation in playing a game of "round the birches". A couple of times she reared up on her hind legs like a horse as though to trample her young adversary. In Johnny's weakened condition he knew he couldn't keep this up much longer so he scampered up the largest of the trees. When the moose understood his move she gave him a boost with her nose—but the help was purely accidental; she really didn't want him out of her reach. The huge beast continued to make threatening motions with her head and hooves, but Johnny was safely out of harm's way. Just when she seemed to be calming down, the calves showed up and she again worked herself into a frenzy. After what seemed like hours the moose gave up and led her calves away.

When Johnny was sure he was safe he crawled down and stretched. Then, as though she had been waiting in ambush, the moose thundered back on the scene. Johnny retreated up the tree, and none too soon. And so there was a repeat performance of pawing and head shaking and brushing against the clump of trees. She didn't stay nearly as long as the first time, but again when Johnny descended she was back. This time he had kept one hand on a substantial branch and the moose wasn't even close by the time he was 10 feet up in the air. Apparently the animal's anger and frustration finally turned to discouragement because this time she left for good. Johnny spent the rest of the day very close to trees he could climb and come dark built himself a cradle like platform in another clump of birches. There was no way he would sleep on the ground with the moose and her calves in the vicinity!

Before going to sleep, Johnny again prayed that he would be given a guardian spirit. As he finally dozed off he was thinking, "It would be just my luck to dream about a moose; after all the trouble they've given me I don't think I could trust a moose-spirit to be on my side."

Shortly after he fell asleep, Johnny moved just right—or just wrong—and awoke with a crash as he landed on the ground flat on his back! He was sure the moose had him. But when there was no attack he finally figured out what had happened and crawled back up to his cradle. This time it was nearly daybreak when he finally dozed off once again. As the sun rose he was still fast asleep. A crow alighted in his tree and began an awful racket—all of which triggered a dream in Johnny's tired brain. He thought he had once again fallen to the ground and the moose calves were attacking him. In his dream he heard crows cawing and imagined that dozens of the big black birds drove off the moose calves and carried him with their beaks to the top of a big pine tree and safety. Then he dreamed he was falling. . .falling. . .falling down through the branches; as he regained consciousness he realized he actually was falling! but this time he was awake enough to grab at the branches as they passed by and broke his fall, actually landing on his feet. As he stood there, leaning against a tree trunk for support and trying to catch his breath, he suddenly realized, "Hey! I've had my dream! The crow is my guardian spirit!"

All that day Johnny searched for a crow feather to put in the deerskin medicine pouch Net-no-kwa had given him before he left the village. He saw several crows' nests but no feathers were to be found on the ground below. Then he had an idea, why not climb one of those trees? There would surely be some feathers in a nest. He retraced his steps to the last one he had seen—in a huge Norway pine with the nest well up towards the top. After resting a considerable time to regain his strength, he began the climb. The possibility of young ones being in the nest had never occurred to him. About half way up an adult crow discovered him and cried out in alarm. Crows came from every where—dozens of them. Their cawing was deafening as they took turns diving at Johnny, coming so close he could easily have hit or kicked several, but he just held on for dear life. Suddenly one of the crows landed in the nest, killed the half grown young one that was there, and pushed it out! The fluttering of the dead bird to the ground was like a signal. The cawing ceased and every crow flew away. Almost sadly, Johnny slid down and picked up the dead bird. Staring at the lifeless form he rationalized, "Maybe it was meant to be."

Anyway, the quest was over. Taking his knife from his belt, Johnny cut off one claw. Then he plucked the longest feather from a wing, and placed them both in his medicine pouch. He was a brave!

CHAPTER IX
LAKE OF THE WOODS

The only one who was in a hurry to leave the village that spring was Net-no-kwa. During the winter she had sought out and become acquainted with a number of families, all related to each other, who were planning to travel to the Red Lake area when the ice went out. She really wasn't anxious to leave her daughter and grandchildren. In fact, she had been tempted to make the village "home", but there were other relatives in the west and she and Tau-ga-we-ninne had planned the move for so long. The delays, problems and frustrations along the way had only made her more determined to achieve her original goal. Once she had reaffirmed her decision to continue, she couldn't wait to be on her way.

As for the boys, they were still enjoying the companionship and expertise of Maji-go-bo in the ways of the wilds. As far as they were concerned, the land of the buffalo could wait.

With the passing of the sugar harvest, the group made their preparations and the day of departure finally came. Good-byes didn't come easy, but the sadness of separation was tempered with anticipation for a country yet unseen.

Rainy River came first and it was magnificent with its exciting Koochiching Falls and broad expanses of water—much of it bordered by stately white and Norway pines. Johnny told his mother, "This is the most beautiful river I have ever seen."

The second night the party made camp at the mouth of the river, on a point, in full view of the Lake of the Woods. The Indians identified it as "Pequona", Lake of the Sand Hills. As a matter of fact, they considered the Lake of the Woods as four separate bodies of water[1]: Lake of the Sand Hills (Big Traverse), Sabaskong Bay, Whitefish Bay and the north end of the lake, including Shoal Lake.

Little did Johnny realize that one day when he was a man with a family of his own, this lake of 14,000 islands would be his home.

Come morning, they broke camp and swung out onto the lake itself, passing the Sable Islands and then out into the big water. There was a choice of routes to the Red River country. One could follow the south shore to the Warroad River, and after traveling south on that stream, take a ten mile portage to Hay River, which feeds into the Roseau River. From there they could travel to the Red River, then north to Lake Winnipeg—or, as the Indians called it,—"Lake of the Dirty Water". However, this route passed closer to Sioux country so this time they chose the alternate way which led to the north end of the Lake of the Woods, where the Winnipeg River would take them west to their destination. It was the intention of the travelers to follow the west side of the Alneau Peninsula on their way north, but heavy winds made them change their minds and they decided to follow the east side instead. By the time the party reached the shelter of what we call "Bigsby Island", waves were breaking over the canoes and Johnny was kept busy bailing with a kettle—just about as fast as he could work.

Rather than go beyond the island and have to fight the heavy waters once more, the travelers selected a sheltered cove on the east side and called it a day. Campfire time meant story telling time and that night Net-no-kwa told the boys, "I had hoped we would travel the other way around the peninsula. I wanted to point out an island held in taboo by the Indian People."

"In taboo?" Johnny asked, "What does "taboo" mean?"

"In this case it means a place of evil where one does not dare go—something bad might happen there. 'Taboo' is something we don't do."

"Well, why not?" pressed the inquisitive Johnny.

"If you will stop interrupting, I will tell you!" Net-no-kwa chided.

She then went on, "Many moons ago, perhaps about the same time those Sioux war parties were back there on Basswood Lake and Lake Saganaga, a group of French voyageur-soldiers were massacred by the Sioux on the little island I was telling you about."

---

[1]In that day the four areas were even more separated because of a nine foot lower water level—there being no dams at the north end of the lake.

"You mean they were all killed?" Wa-me-gon-a-biew asked.

"Yes, all of them."

"Where did they come from? Where were they going?" It was Johnny's turn to ask.

"In those days there was a big fort on this lake about a half-day's journey west of the island of taboo I was telling you about. These men were a part of a much larger company who were stationed at the fort. Where they were going, I do not know."

"Are all places taboo where people get killed?" was Johnny's next question.

"No, not usually," Net-no-kwa replied, "but in this case there was a holy man traveling with the whites, and it is feared his powerful spirit will punish any Indian who sets foot on the island."

"Would we have seen the fort if we had gone the other way?" Johnny asked.

"I don't think so; I understand it would be out of our way. It is west of the regular route to the north end of the lake, but it is no longer in use and there probably isn't much to see there now, anyway."

Net-no-kwa was right. When Alexander Henry, the explorer, had passed that way a few years earlier (1775) he found it to be abandoned and described it as "an old French trading house. . .almost everything being destroyed by the Nadowessies (Sioux)."

Actually the place Net-no-kwa had in mind was historic Fort St. Charles, founded by the famous French-Canadian explorer, Pierre La Verendrye in 1732. He and his four sons had used this as their base of operations as they explored and mapped central Canada, even going southwest as far as the Black Hills and northwest into Saskatchewan. They constructed seven forts in all, including fort St. Pierre on Rainy Lake and Fort Maurepas on the Red River, which was later moved to the Winnipeg River. La Verendrye's oldest son, Jean Baptiste, had been the leader of the group of 21 who had been massacred by the Sioux in 1736. The priest was Father Alneau, and the huge peninsula the travelers were working their way around would one day be named in honor of this martyr.

That night, Johnny and Wa-me-gon-a-biew went to sleep trying to visualize the bloody attack and wondering how many Sioux were killed before the last Frenchman died.

The next day, the wind had subsided and the small band continued in a northeasterly direction, passing some painted rocks about noon. The caravan continued through a maze of islands, finally stopping on a beach near the tip of Rabbit Point just off the Alneau Peninsula, and there they made camp for the night.

The ideal campsite proved to be a place of misfortune for the tragedy-plagued Net-no-kwa. As she climbed a hillside looking for firewood, she slipped on a moss-covered rock, wedging her foot into a crack in the rocks as she fell. She broke her leg just above the ankle. It was an ugly break and extremely painful. One of the older braves who professed some experience in setting broken bones came to her aid. He did a fine job, but Net-no-kwa fainted in the process. It was just as well. By the time she came to, four sturdy splints had been lashed around her leg. A stretcher was made from a blanket and she was gently born back down to the campsite. The pain was bad enough in itself, but Net-no-kwa was emotionally upset and depressed at the prospect of making the rest of the long journey in her handicapped condition. It was a sleepless night.

Come morning, the boys broke camp and with the help of their fellow travelers managed to lift Net-no-kwa into their canoe. But no position was comfortable, and the rough waters of a windy day added to her misery. By the time they reached the narrow channel that leads from Sabaskong Bay into Turtle Lake—where the Whitefish portage is only a mile or so away—Net-no-kwa made a decision. She announced, "The boys and I will have to stay behind."

She told the leadership, "It is no use; I cannot travel farther. You must go on. There will be other tribes to pass this way after I am well again. We will join one of them and still make it to Red River by freeze-up."

With genuine reluctance, the group pulled over to the little island by the entrance to the Turtle Lake channel. Most everyone pitched in to provide the family with enough food to last a couple of weeks if necessary. The small island was chosen as the campsite so that if the boys took off hunting or fishing, Net-no-kwa wouldn't have to worry about some roving bear or other animal. It was also strategically located on the main north-south route for that part of the lake where they could easily intercept any group traveling to the Red River area once Net-no-kwa was well enough to travel again.

With plenty of time on their hands, the boys developed a comfortable campsite. But Net-no-kwa was depressed. It seemed as though everything that could go wrong—did.

On the second afternoon Johnny and Wa-me-gon-a-biew set out the family fish net, directly in front of the lodge. The next morning they could see the net was "active" and as they pulled it, they retrieved more than a dozen walleyes and about half that many northerns. There would be plenty of fresh fish. Nevertheless, a few days later as the boys were exploring for rice beds in which to hunt ducks, they were fishing again—this time trolling a baited hook on a handline tied to the gunwale of their canoe. Suddenly, the boat literally stopped dead. The boys' first thought that they had hooked bottom. Just then the water exploded far back of the canoe and one of the biggest fish they had ever seen broke completely out of the water.

"A muskie!" Wa-me-gon-a-biew yelled.

In the half hour which followed, there were times the boys weren't sure who was catching whom as the big fish literally dragged the light canoe where it pleased, frequently breaking water and shaking its massive head in an attempt to throw the hook. But it finally wore itself out and the boys were able to beach their canoe and work the big lunker into the shallows. Once they had it up on the dry sand, Wa-me-gon-a-biew straddled the muskie and tried to sit on it to keep the fish from squirming back into the water. As the monster continued to flop it actually lifted the teenager off the ground! But the outcome was no longer in doubt—the prize was theirs. It proved to be about as long as Johnny was tall and weighed over 30 pounds—maybe 40. Even Net-no-kwa was cheered by the enthusiastic account of every detail of the battle.

The next day was devoted to pot-shooting mallards in a rice bed the boys had discovered through the channel in Turtle Lake. They didn't have the heart to shoot the hens who were still attending their young broods but had a great time picking off the greenheaded drakes. As they returned to camp the boys were in for a surprise—a virtual parade of canoes, all filled with braves, making its way from the east in the direction of the island, coming down the channel between Hay Island and the mainland. A bit jittery, Johnny and Wa-me-gon-a-biew weren't sure whether they were in trouble or not.

"What do you think, Wa-me-gon-a-biew? Shall we make a run for it and distract them from the island? Maybe we can hide if we hurry!"

"It's too late," the Indian boy replied, "They have surely seen us and we wouldn't have a chance. We'd be better off to paddle out to meet them as though we had no reason to be afraid."

"That's easy for you to say." Johnny responded. "I'm in the bow and I'd be the first one to get it if they intend to do us harm."

"Don't you think they'd get me, too?" Wa-me-gon-a-biew argued.

"I suppose you're right." Johnny admitted. "I guess there really isn't any choice. Let's go."

The boys paddled leisurely into the path of the oncoming armada. They didn't have long to wait. As the first canoe pulled alongside the boys searched the faces of the braves in vain for some sign of friendliness. They just didn't look very happy.

Wa-me-gon-a-biew quickly extended a greeting, but it was ignored as the grim faced man in the stern of the lead canoe spoke, "We were wondering who had invaded our hunting grounds. Where is your tribe?"

"There is just us boys and our mother who has a broken leg and is on that island," Wa-me-gon-a-biew said, pointing.

"We shall see," the man answered soberly, dipping his paddle urgently as he turned his face towards the island.

Net-no-kwa had observed the whole proceedings and was waiting at water's edge, leaning on the crutch her oldest son had made for her. The remarkable woman was in command of every situation and this was no exception. The crutch only dignified her queenly bearing as she asked with a smile, "Do you come to invade my island kingdom or to strike an alliance against our mutual enemies?"

The stone-faced chief (he turned out to be the head chief of the village) allowed the corners of his mouth to turn up just a little and spoke, "I see it is as the boys have said. How did you get here? And what happened to you?"

"My sons and I were traveling with a band of Ojibway from Rainy Lake and were headed for Red River, When I slipped on a rock while gathering firewood and broke my leg. The pain was too much and we decided to wait here, hoping another band will come along that we may join when I feel better. My sons are too young and I am too old to travel by ourselves in a strange land."

"Our village is just around the point that marks the end of this channel." the chief explained as he pointed to the east. "There is no need for you to stay here by yourselves; you are welcome to return with us to our village."

"Your kindness is appreciated," Net-no-kwa replied, "But we don't want to miss any group traveling our way—and they must pass this island if they are going north."

"There is no problem," the chief assured her. "In the first place, you cannot travel for a long time yet. Meanwhile, my men are on the lake every day and they will surely encounter such a group."

The thought crossed Net-no-kwa's mind that she and the boys had been here several days and had not been "encountered" by the chief's men, but she appreciated the security of the village and said with a smile, "Very well then, my sons and I accept your kind offer."

As the boys broke camp, one of the braves pointed at Johnny but addressed Net-no-kwa, "You say 'your sons' but this one must have been kept in the dark all his life to have so pale a countenance!"

Everyone laughed and Net-no-kwa explained how she had come to be Johnny's mother.

The village was located on the mainland and included about fifty lodges. It was located on a gently sloping hillside with a spectacular view of the lake, enhanced by numerous wooded islands so characteristic of Sabaskong Bay. The inhabitants were Ojibway—a friendly people who made the Ottawa family feel very much at home. The framework of an abandoned lodge was made available to them and by nightfall the boys had it well covered with blankets, skins and bark.

It was here that Johnny learned more about medicine as practiced by the Indians—first hand. Shortly after their arrival, Johnny was eating his evening meal—too fast as usual—and swallowed a cartilage-like sturgeon bone. Somehow it caught crosswise in his esophagus, causing much discomfort. When he tried to swallow, nothing would go down, and coughing would not bring it up.

A neighbor woman volunteered, "We have a powerful shaman in our village who is among those who heals by sucking troublesome objects right out of the body through the skin. Shall I summon him?"

Net-no-kwa had heard of this practice, but was a little dubious.

The neighbor woman persisted, "With my own eyes I have seen him suck a fish bone out of a man's neck and a water hair shake out of a girl's stomach!"

Johnny was in obvious discomfort and Net-no-kwa did not wish to offend the well-meaning neighbor, so she nodded her assent, adding, "We will try it, please call him."

While waiting for the medicine man to arrive, Net-no-kwa assured Johnny, "Do not worry Little Falcon, he cannot hurt you—and who knows. . .?" She added the last phrase with a shrug of her shoulders.

Johnny really had his doubts but his level of confidence diminished even further when the Shaman turned out to be a very wierd looking man, bent with age, and virtually toothless when he smiled. He wore a brass ring in his nose and a heavy ear ornament made of metal, cone-shaped objects.

Before examining his patient, the medicine man turned to Net-no-kwa and negotiated her promise that if he were successful she would make him a pair of high-topped winter moccasins, lined with rabbit fur. She agreed when he gave her full assurance that he would expect nothing if he could not heal her son.

The bargain struck, the old man directed Johnny to lie down on his back. He then produced a wide, membrane-thin section of a bone. It was so thin it was porous enough to suck air right through it. This was laid on the spot at the base of the neck where Johnny had indicated the bone was lodged. The medicine man then lay on his stomach at right angles to his patient, placed his mouth against the bone and began to suck. Johnny could feel the drawing sensation on his neck. It was a noisy process and if he weren't so miserable and still half scared he would probably have laughed. In fact, as he watched Wa-me-gon-a-biew out of the corner of his eye he was sure his brother was snickering!

After a great deal of time had passed, perhaps an hour, Johnny suddenly felt tremendous relief as the bone dislodged. The Shaman staggered to his feet and in a gesture of triumph, produced a piece of bone he claimed to have sucked right through his patient's skin! It looked suspiciously like the knuckle end of a partridge leg to Net-no-kwa, but she was so relieved her son was all right that she didn't mind assuring the old man the moccasins would be delivered in a few days. As for Johnny, he couldn't figure out how the bone could come out through his skin without leaving a hole and, besides, he could have sworn he felt the bone moving down his digestive track. But one thing was sure, he promised himself he would eat more slowly and chew his food more carefully in the future.

Meanwhile, Net-no-kwa's leg continued to heal nicely. In fact, so well she not only discarded the crutch but even threw away the splints—and that was a mistake. She had joined some other women from the village in a blueberry picking expedition on one of the larger islands—the Indians actually called it "Blueberry Island". Their job done and their birchbark baskets heaped full with the little, round juicy berries—the women were about to leave the island. Net-no-kwa just didn't see the wet moss on the flat rock at the water's edge and as she raised one foot to step into the canoe—down she went—so fast there was no way she could break her fall. The bone had mended, but it just wasn't strong enough to withstand the jolt. Net-no-kwa was furious with herself for being so careless. Back at the village, Johnny and Wa-me-gon-a-biew didn't help matters any. In fact, they enjoyed the rare opportunity of lecturing their mother for her impatience and carelessness.

The annual Rendezvous at Grand Portage had come and gone, and several "convoys" of canoes glided among the islands of Sabaskong Bay on their way north, but Net-no-kwa was in no position to travel and the reports of tribes on the move only added to her frustration. Her anxieties were only slightly eased when the village chief (Skwek-o-mik) promised to send word back to Win-et-ka and Maji-go-bo on Rainy Lake, telling them of her plight. She felt a little better when word came back that there would be a group from the village going to Red River at ice-out in the spring and they would stop by to pick up the trouble-plagued family on their way. Meanwhile, Net-no-kwa, Wa-me-gon-a-biew and Johnny tried to look forward to a winter in the little village on Sabaskong Bay.

But first came fall and hunting, something both boys totally enjoyed. The most memorable experience that autumn for either Johnny or Wa-me-gon-a-biew took place during a moose hunting expedition to the south shore of Sabaskong Bay. The boys joined a small party of hunters on invitation from Chief Skwek-o-mik himself, and left the village on a perfect October morning. It was one of those days in the northland when the sky was cloudless turquois blue. There was just enough crispness in the air to make the boys glad they were paddling so as to keep warm. The yellow birch and aspen leaves which had already begun to fall collected like gold on the flat rocks along the shore. The annual waterfowl migration was underway and several times during the day they heard the honking of geese and the trumpeting of swans, and Johnny and Wa-me-gon-a-biew made a game of seeing who would be first to spot them. The snow geese and the longnecked swans were especially beautiful as they contrasted against the solid blue sky. It was an exhilarating morning; a day when you were glad to be alive.

The canoe parties traveled in silence. The hunters hoped to see a moose along the way. Several times, one or more of the canoe parties left the procession to explore deep bays or check the opposite sides of islands for feeding animals. By noon the hunters had worked their way to Nestor Falls, at the east end of Sabaskong Bay, without seeing a single moose—or deer either, for that matter. They had not expected to see caribou, because they had just begun their migration south. Deer were scarce for another reason: they competed poorly with the moose for food. This was particularly true in winter when the larger animals could stretch their thick necks and pick off cedar boughs or anything else edible, far beyond the reach of deer.

The hunters went to shore at Nestor Falls, and Chief Skwek-o-mik called to Johnny and Wa-me-gon-a-biew, "Find some frogs and I will show you how to catch some big walleyes for our noon meal." In a matter of minutes, the boys were back with nearly a dozen frogs' heads peering out from between their fingers.

"Stand here," the chief directed, pointing to a flat shelf of granite at the water's edge. "Throw your handline out just a little way. It is deep right off shore—maybe 10 or 12 feet—just let the frog settle to the bottom."

Before either boy's frog had reached bottom their lines started moving out from shore. "Either your frogs are very strong swimmers or else you both have a bite!" the chief exclaimed, "Set the hook!"

Johnny gave a yank and when the walleye felt the barb, it really took off; Wa-me-gon-a-biew's did the same. It was not easy battling a big fish by hand. One didn't dare pull too hard or the line might break, or if you gave the fish slack he would throw the hook. Worst of all, if the line were allowed to run out too fast it would burn the skin between your fingers. But the boys had learned their lessons well—the hard way—and soon two big bellied walleyes were slid flopping out onto the flat rock. Their size was almost identical—seven or eight pounds at least—and the boys argued off and on all during lunch as to whose was the bigger. Other hunters-turned-fishermen were also having good luck and in a matter of minutes had more fish than they could eat.

It was highly unlikely moose would come down to the water at midday so the chief suggested everyone take a nap, "Because," he advised, "if we don't have any luck by dark we will have to hunt by moonlight."

When the hunt was resumed late that afternoon, a cow was spotted in Gohere Bay. While the lead canoe silently approached the feeding animal, the rest of the canoes remained out beyond the moose's vision. Most animals are much less concerned about what happens out on the water in front of them than back in the woods. By paddling quietly and nosing the canoe straight at the moose, the hunters were able to approach even within arrow range. However, this time they would use the muzzle-loader rather than take a chance on wounding the huge beast and having to trail it far back into the brush and then have the very difficult job of packing the meat out to the shore. The boys waited in anticipation; they seemed so close! After an eternity, the brave in the bow raised his gun. There was a huge puff of smoke, the moose fell with a splash, and then they heard the shot.

A second canoe was sent in to help with the butchering. When an animal weighs a half ton and has to be worked out of the water before it can be cut up, it helps to have plenty of manpower.

Chief Skwek-o-mik turned to Johnny and Wa-me-gon-a-biew and told them, "You may as well go on into Splitrock Bay, the second bay up the shore," he said, pointing. "It will soon be dark. If there is nothing there, pull into shore and wait. The moon is already up and it will be light enough to shoot all night. You may not be able to see the moose when he comes down to the lake, but you should be able to hear him when he wades in and when he feeds. If you grow weary of waiting, paddle quietly around the bay; it is just possible you may not hear one come down. Even with a bright moon it will be hard to see your sights, so go in very close before firing. And most important of all, watch the wind so they will not smell you."

"What if we get one?" Johnny asked.

"We will hear you shoot and come to help." was the reply.

"If we don't shoot a moose, how long should we wait?"

"Until I come for you. I will call like an owl just in case you are sneaking up on a moose. But do not fall asleep or you will not hear me and we will be waiting for nothing." As the boys started to paddle away, the chief added, "Do not be surprised if we do not come for you until after daybreak; that is the best hunting time, you know."

It was getting dark as Johnny and Wa-me-gon-a-biew nosed their canoe around the point and into Splitrock Bay, but there was nothing in sight.

"Let's paddle around the bay anyway," Wa-me-gon-a-biew whispered. "There could be one back in the rushes or just coming down to the lake."

Johnny nodded and they leisurely and silently worked their way around the circumference, but the only life they saw was a pair of loons playing out in the middle and a lone beaver towing a freshly cut aspen branch along the shore near the waterfall at the far end of the bay. Before it became totally dark, the boys headed for a vantage point with a grassy bank where they could wait it out.

The night was full of noises, highlighted by the plaintive and ghostly call of the loons as they communicated with another pair out on the main lake. Flocks of migrating ducks whirred overhead and sometimes could be heard splashing down for a rest. Occasionally a mallard would quack in one of the many pockets of rice along the shore. Once, the almost human cry of a lynx directly back in the woods gave the boys

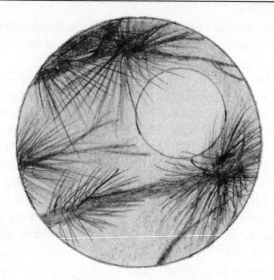

goosebumps and made the hair on the backs of their necks feel like it was standing on end. On a far off hill a timber wolf howled at the moon and still farther away another gave its reply. The moon gave everything a soft, erie glow and its reflection sparkled on the ripples in the bay, while in the northern sky the aurora borealis began its display of dancing lights. It was a very special night and a very special experience.

The boys began to grow sleepy and fought to keep their eyes open. They had long since given up on a moose making an appearance. Wa-me-gon-a-biew suggested, "Little Falcon, why don't you go to sleep; I will take the first watch."

"You talked me into it," Johnny replied, "But when are you going to stop calling me "*Little* Falcon?""

"When you are big enough to stop me!" was the smart retort.

"Don't worry, that day will come." Johnny promised. Although the white boy knew he was finally catching up to his Indian brother—in both height and weight—he also knew the time to challenge him was

still a long way off. Even when Wa-me-gon-a-biew would let him start on top in their brotherly wrestling matches, he never stayed there very long. So when Wa-me-gon-a-biew gave him a friendly push over backwards from his sitting position, he was content to stay on his back and try to sleep.

Johnny had just dozed off when Wa-me-gon-a-biew grabbed his arm and whispered, "Listen!"

Johnny sat upright—fully awake. They both heard it—the unmistakable splashing and gurgling of an animal entering the lake, and not very far down the shore.

Silently, the boys descended to the water's edge, slipped their canoe into the lake, and with muffled paddles worked their way in the direction of the noise. The wind was favorable—no danger of the moose smelling them. Johnny suddenly realized there was no longer a moon; a heavy overcast had moved in and the night had become very black. He wondered if they would be able to see the animal. All they could do in the meantime was work towards the noise. It sounded as though whatever it was submerged its head while feeding, because every once in awhile they could hear a boiling noise like a head coming out of the water, and for a minute or so afterwards there would be little splashing sounds of water trickling back into the lake. It seemed like they were very near. Now they could make out the profile of towering spruce trees against the sky; they were so close to the shore and yet the sound had to be between them and the trees! But still no moose.

Suddenly, with the violence of an erupting volcano—right alongside the canoe—the enormous antlered head of a bull moose came out of the water. They could have touched him! Before either could fire, the moose—suddenly aware of his predicament—rose up on his hind legs, towering above the canoe and its occupants. Both boys shot from the hip and the monster came crashing down. As the moose fell, one antler caught the canoe midway between Johnny and Wa-me-gon-a-biew, ripping through the birchbark as though it were paper! The boys suddenly found themselves in neck-deep ice water—but unhurt. By instinct, they had both held on to their muzzle loaders. The moose was obviously—and fortunately—dead. They dragged what was left of their canoe out of the water and then tried to maneuver their huge trophy towards shore. Because the water considerably reduced the animal's weight they were able to work it in a few feet from where it dropped, but that was all. About that time they decided a fire and getting dried out were more important. It wasn't easy finding birchbark and dry wood in the darkness, but by the time the first canoes of their fellow hunters entered the bay, they had a roaring fire going with the aid of their ever-reliable flint and steel.

The boys told their story to their hunting companions with mixed embarrassment and pride. Chief Skwek-o-mik declared the canoe beyond repair, but promised to help the boys build a replacement after their return.

Back at the village, Net-no-kwa reminded Johnny that this was his third serious encounter with a moose and gave him a motherly lecture about being more careful.

★   ★   ★

Winter was late in coming to the northland that year—but when it came, it was with a vengeance. First the heavy snows—blizzard after blizzard, and then the bitter cold—day after day. It was soon nearly im-possible to hunt very far from the village; the snow was so light and powdery even snowshoes helped little. To make matters worse, the game near the village had been pretty well trapped or shot out years before. The tribe worked hard to keep their ice holes open for netting, but they had been cut too close to shore and before the winter was very old the combination of the dropping water level and the thickening ice (over three feet) left little room for the fish to swim between the bottom of the ice and the bottom of the lake.

Johnny thought the winter at Grand Portage had been tough, but this was much worse. With spring still weeks away the entire village faced starvation. Fish and game were so scarce families resorted to making soups and broths from almost anything that would provide nourish-ment. Old animal and fish bones were boiled again and again. From past experiences, the villagers had learned there was some nourish-ment to be found in the inner bark of the pine tree and that the lichen could be scraped from rocks and brewed into a dark, glue-like pudding. The boys complained about the horrible taste of both, but Net-no-kwa wisely insisted, "If you do not eat, you will surely become sick with some disease."

Indeed, a few of the older villagers did die that winter. Most prayed daily to the Great Spirit for help in finding game, but hunting expedi-tions remained unsuccessful. One by one, the village dogs were eaten as a last resort.

Net-no-kwa had always had a reputation for divining the location of animals but was hesitant to practive her art among strangers lest she should fail. However, faced with starvation, she prayed herself into a trance and indeed had a vision. She saw a family of three moose—a cow, a calf and a bull—yarded up by a frozen beaver pond. Net-no-kwa wanted to report her dream, but there were so many beaver ponds the braves would only laugh at her. So again she prayed, and the next night she had much the same vision, only this time she was shown a beaver dam in an unusual location—between two steep hillsides. In spite of her fears that hunters would not find any moose and that she would then be disgraced, she determined to share her visions with the chief himself. After many apologies for being so bold as to make a suggestion, Net-no-kwa told him, "All my days I have had a gift for medicine hunting. On several occasions when game was scarce the Great Spirit has given me a vision of where animals might be found. In the last few days I have fasted and prayed and twice the Great Spirit has shown me a family of three moose near a beaver pond."

"But Net-no-kwa," Chief Skwek-o-mik interrupted, "There are so many beaver ponds."

"I know," the Indian woman replied, "but in the second vision I saw the beaver had built their dam in a narrow passage between two steep hillsides. The hills themselves were not very large, but the sides were very steep where the dam was built."

The chief raised one eyebrow, "I know such a place. It is not far from here. The dam is on a small creek that flows from a pond into Turtle Lake." But then he added warily, "I must tell you that our men were there not long ago and saw nothing."

"Perhaps you and my sons could go; then if I am wrong, no one will know. I would be so humiliated after the many kindnesses the village people have shown me and my sons."

"So shall it be." The chief assured her.

Net-no-kwa had not shared her dreams with the boys; she had not wanted to burden them with so serious a decision. But upon her return to the lodge she told them the whole story and that she had approach-ed the chief and he was willing to take them with him. To her surprise and hurt Wa-me-gon-a-biew was angry.

"Remember, Mother, you have not always been right. If we go all that way through snow up to our chests and don't find game, the chief may be so angry he will kill us all!"

Wa-me-gon-a-biew was serious. Net-no-kwa had not given that possibility a thought and she was immediately sorry for her intervention, "But it is too late my son. It is all arranged. If such be the case that I am wrong, we will have to throw ourselves at his mercy. He seems a good man."

Johnny just couldn't imagine such a reprisal and reminded his brother, "Think of the times he has taken us with him hunting and how he helped us build a new canoe."

The discussion ended abruptly when Chief Skwek-o-mik's deep voice was heard at the entrance to the lodge, "Forgive me for listening in on your family argument, but you have nothing to fear."

The chief lifted the heavy moosehide that covered the doorway and stepped inside.

"Net-no-kwa, you were a brave woman to come to me. Our situation is so desperate it is well worth the try. Besides, even with the deep snow, it will be less than a two hours' journey."

With a rare but reassuring smile he turned to Johnny and Wa-me-gon-a-biew and asked, "Are you boys ready?"

The lack of proper nourishment had taken its toll and the hunters stopped many times to rest. Chief Skwek-o-mik and Wa-me-gon-a-biew took turns breaking trail. The muzzle-loaders were so heavy and the walking so difficult—but they made it. They first saw the frozen pond at the opposite end from where the dam was located. Nothing could have looked more devoid of life. As they stood there, a lone raven flew over the clearing, its melodious call sounding like a jeer—taunting the hunters for their silly journey.

"As long as we have come this far," the chief whispered, "we may as well walk around the pond."

This would be no easy task. Though not wide, the pond was a good half mile long, and it meant staying well back in the woods to keep out of sight. Painfully they worked their way up a little hill to get a better view. As Chief Skwek-o-mik peered cautiously over the top he suddenly froze, and then ever so slowly, slid back down. When he turned around his normally expressionless face was split from ear to ear with a big grin. He held up three fingers!

Using extreme caution, the chief led the boys back down the hillside and around its base. Fallen trees and dry branches were carefully avoided. Every step was taken with care, testing for potential noise problems before putting their full weight down—even though the deep snow would have helped muffle most noises. At long last he motioned for the boys to take their places beside him so that each could have an open shot. The boys knew from experience the hunter to the left would shoot the animal to the left, the hunter to the right would take the animal to the right, and so on. When all was ready, the chief gave a nod and they raised up, ever so slowly, to peer over the snow-covered rocky ridge which lay like a rampart just in front of them. Afterwards, Wa-me-gon-a-biew would say, "It was like shooting fish in a puddle!"

There they were: an antlerless bull, a cow and a calf, contentedly chewing on cedar boughs, completely unaware of any danger. The trampled "yard" showed they have been there for some time—at least a couple of weeks. Chief Skwek-o-mik again nodded and all three raised their muzzle-loaders. Johnny was weak with fatigue and excitement. Luckily there was the stump of a fallen tree immediately in front of him on which he could rest his wavering gun barrel. He fired first; the more experienced hunters had waited, not wanting the sound of their shots to throw off his aim. The animals crumpled right where they stood: one - two - three! Even if they had missed or wounded the moose, the snow was so deep even these long legged beasts would not have gone far before the hunters could have reloaded.

Before the first animal was half butchered the starving hunters cut off pieces of tripe to chew on as they worked. Later, Wa-me-gon-a-biew built a fire and the chief sliced off thick steaks which Johnny pinned on some sticks and broiled over the blazing fire—not even waiting for coals to form. The fast was broken!

The triumphant trio returned, each dragging a front quarter behind him. The journey back was far easier, and as they stepped into the clearing at the top of the hill and looked down on the village, Chief Skwek-o-mik shouted the good news at the top of his voice. In minutes every able-bodied person was on the way to carry home every morsel of meat and bone before night would fall and before wolves or other predators might find the meat.

The chief saved his announcement of how they had discovered the moose for an evening council fire. Dramatically, he praised Net-no-kwa and her sons—even telling of their fear of reprisal should the hunt have been in vain. Chief Skwek-o-mik ended his oration by proclaiming, "The Great Spirit has sent this family to us. See how he has rewarded all of us for our hospitality towards them? Let it be a lesson—may we never deny a kindness to anyone in need. Now let us all give prayers of praise and thanksgiving to the Great Spirit."

With those words, the chief lifted his hands and his voice to his Kit-chi Manitou and everyone joined in.

By the time the three moose had been consumed, there was a promise of spring in the air. The March sun had crusted the drifts and it was once again possible to use snowshoes and hunt at a much greater distance from the village. But Net-no-kwa and her two sons—the one Red, the other White—would be remembered by this village for many moons.

CHAPTER X
RED RIVER AT LAST

Faithful to their word, a tiny band of Rainy Lake Indians, six canoes in all, stopped at the Sabaskong Bay village one June day to pick up Net-no-kwa and her sons and take them along to the Red River. One of the braves noticed how much Johnny had grown in a year's time and asked, "How old are you now, Little Falcon?"

"Fifteen summers!" He replied quickly, with obvious pride and in a voice that had finally changed for keeps.

Indeed, more than his voice had changed. Johnny's natural parents would never have recognized the tall, straight-backed, deep-chested, broad-shouldered young man they had last seen as a scrawny 10-year-old. His once pudgy face was now strikingly handsome and his lighter hair and blue eyes set him clearly apart from his Indian family and friends. Already a head taller than his mother and dead-even with Wa-me-gon-a-biew, he took every opportunity to walk on higher ground so that he could look down just a little on his Indian brother. Wa-me-gon-a-biew wasn't exactly happy at the prospect of having his younger brother become his bigger brother and used his greater strength on many more occasions than absolutely necessary to remind Johnny that he was still boss.

While Net-no-kwa and the boys packed, the Rainy Lake Indians enjoyed a day of rest before resuming the journey. The villagers, with the heroics of their three visitors during the past winter still fresh on their minds, were deeply emotional in their farewells. Chief Skwek-o-mik, his blanket draped over his left arm, almost as a symbol of his authority, gave quite an oration which ended: "As long as the sun rises over our heads and as long as the water runs in our rivers and streams, the story of how this family, with the help of the Great Spirit, saved us from starving to death, shall be told around the campfires of our village."

He then presented the family with gifts. The boys each received an ash bow and a half-dozen arrows and Net-no-kwa a pair of beaded moccasins. The Chief explained that the bow strings were special: they were made from sinews taken from snapping turtles and would not stretch or shrink.

As Net-no-kwa took one last look back at the village and then turned to face the future, she couldn't help but wonder what would happen next to keep her from reaching the Red River country.

Within minutes the procession passed the little island where the family camped when Net-no-kwa had broken her leg. Next, they passed through the channel leading to Turtle Lake, where the narrow, green leaves of the new rice crop were already floating on the water. Families of ducks were everywhere, as though anticipating the rice harvest still nearly three months away.

The leader of the group, Mik-e-nuk, let his canoe drop back alongside that of the newest members and with "tongue-in-cheek" proclaimed to the boys, "This lake is named for me!"

In Ojibway, his name did indeed mean "turtle," but the truth of the matter was that the shallow lake was home for many a big "snapper" and thereby derived its name. At the north end of the lake, they passed a deserted trading post as they made their short portage into beautiful Whitefish Bay. Johnny looked down into the deep, clear waters and observed, "The Indians are surely right in saying this is a different lake from Sabaskong. Even the islands are not the same."

As the travelers proceeded up the long, winding bay, slipping past island after island, they met several canoes of voyageurs bound for the Rendezvous at Grand Portage. Johnny began to feel a little self conscious as the Frenchmen obviously took note of his light complexion and blond hair—often giving him a special greeting as they passed, no doubt wondering what this young White was doing in a caravan of Indians.

As they neared the Three Sisters area, the canoes slowed their pace and handlines were let out in hope of catching lake trout, but the surface water was already too warm and the lakers had sought greater comfort 100 feet or more farther down. When an hour had passed and no one even had a strike, they steered closer to the shoreline and managed to pick up several northerns in the shallower water. A fairly strong west wind discouraged the Indians from leaving the shelter of the bay and entering the more open portion of the lake, so camp was set up on Yellow Girl Point about mid-afternoon.

Remembering his mother's accident the previous year, Johnny considerately told Net-no-kwa, "You stay in camp, Wa-me-gon-a-biew and I will gather the firewood."

"Speak for yourself!" Wa-me-gon-a-biew snorted, "Squaw's work . . uhh!" and he stalked off to get better acquainted with the other braves.

Over supper fire Net-no-kwa told her sons, "This is the part of the lake where gold may be found."

Immediately Johnny's eyes lit up and in his usual manner, fired off a series of questions before his mother could answer the first:

"Where do you look for gold?"

"How do you mine it?"

"Have you ever found any gold?"

Net-no-kwa took a deep breath, and then explained, "Gold is found in the rocks; it is easiest to see in the strips of white quartz. One must break the rock with an iron tomahawk. My first husband and I once found a little gold while visiting Rainy Lake.'

That was all Johnny and Wa-me-gon-a-biew wanted to know. With supper out of the way and several hours of daylight left, they jumped into the canoe and took off to find their fortune. No one ever caught the fever faster than Johnny and Wa-me-gon-a-biew. The boys walked the rocky shores at a torrid pace; their eyes darting from rock to rock but pausing to examine more carefully every vein of quartz. Any bit of yellow coloring caused Johnny's heart to skip a beat. It was nearly dark when Wa-me-gon-a-biew yelled, "Little Falcon, look here! I've found gold!"

Johnny was at his brother's side in a couple of bounds and stared hypnotically at the yellowish metallic flakes he held in his hand. Wa-me-gon-a-biew had chipped them from a dark rock the size of his fist. Hastily they searched the area, sometimes on their hands and knees, but trying to cover as much ground as possible before total darkness set in. Just as they were about to give up, Wa-me-gon-a-biew cried out again, "More gold!" and held up another rock.

The brothers talked excitedly as they paddled back to camp. Wa-me-gon-a-biew speculated, "When we show the others what we have found, surely they will agree to stay here for a few days."

"Gold mining could be much more profitable than trapping." Johnny pointed out. "Maybe we should all stay here for the rest of the summer."

"Right!" Wa-me-gon-a-biew agreed. "Furs aren't prime now anyway, so what's the hurry of getting to the Red River?"

The canoes were still a long way from shore when the boys proclaimed to the campers and to the whole world, "We've found gold!"

Everyone came running and then escorted the boys to the nearest
campfire to examine their find. Mik-e-nuk turned the metallic flakes
over and over in the palm of his big hand and examined them by the
light of the fire—then looked into the faces of the excited boys and said
with a smile, "Fool's gold!"

"What?" both brothers asked in unison.

"Fool's gold," Mik-e-nuk repeated. "It is not gold but mica—it is of no
value."

The boys were crushed, and the laughter of the adults didn't help
any. Quietly they slipped back to their campfire—"their tails between
their legs." The boys sat in silence by the dying embers—their dreams
shattered. Johnny was first to recover and he muttered, just loud
enough so he was sure Wa-me-gon-a-biew could hear him, "Fools gold.
That's a good name for it all right. Look who found it."

With a war whoop Wa-me-gon-a-biew was on him and before
Johnny could close his mouth he was face down in the sand. When his
Indian brother finally let him up, he was still spitting gravel.

"Be careful what you spit out, Little Falcon, You may have gold between your teeth!"

As they broke camp the next morning, the boys were once again
talking of some day returning to Whitefish Bay and resuming their
search. They would have been even more determined had they known
whitemen would have five major gold mining operations going on the
lake before the end of the next century.

The morning winds were light and the canoes proceeded without
problem to Rat Portage. Here at the north end of the lake, they found a
fairly large encampment of Ojibway. As they visited around the village
that evening they learned that this was a spring trapping camp where
the tribe came each year in pursuit of muskrat furs. There were huge
sloughs and overflows just north of the lake which were dotted with
scores of rat houses. Trapping had been good and they were preparing
to take these pelts along with their winter fur harvest to the trading post
on Rainy Lake in time for them to then be sent on to the Rendezvous.

Johnny and Wa-me-gon-a-biew would live to see the day (1836)
when Rat Portage would be the scene of one of the major operations of
the Hudson's Bay Company. It would later be the site of the present
day twin cities of Kewatin and Kenora. Exciting years would follow of

gold mining, railroading, logging and flour mill operations. Three dams would eventually control the natural spillways where the lake pours itself into the Winnipeg River.

Come morning, the travelers launched their canoes into that wide stream and resumed their journey west. They made much better time paddling with the current and in the shelter of the pines and river banks the wind was never a problem. Net-no-kwa found it hard to believe that after three years she was so close to her goal. Four days after leaving the Lake of the Woods the party set up camp near Fort Maurepas at the mouth of the river on the shores of gigantic Lake Winnipeg—called "Lake of Dirty Water" by the Indians because of its murky color, in contrast to the clear waters of the lakes to the east as well as those farther north and west.

Strangely, seeing Lake Winnipeg and knowing that her relatives were probably somewhere on the far shore, Net-no-kwa experienced a melancholy feeling. Heavy west winds kept the party from crossing the lake for several days, and this gave her too much time to think, to remember and to brood. So much had happened since she and Tau-ga-we-ninne had started west with such high hopes and dreams. Not only had she lost her beloved husband, but Kewatin, too, was gone—her bright-eyed, fun-loving Kewatin. And then Wa-net-ka's first husband had died and, because she had remarried, had chosen to stay on a Rainy Lake rather than move west with the rest of the family. All of that would have been tragedy enough, but in addition, a whole year had been lost because of her own carelessness in breaking and then re-breaking her leg. She thought, "What a burden I have been to my sons."

As Net-no-kwa's sorrow and anger fed on each other, she grew more and more depressed, until she did something she had strongly disapproved of all her life—she yielded to the temptation of joining her traveling companions in drinking while waiting for the weather to improve. They seemed to be having so much fun while she felt worse and worse. She told herself, "Why shouldn't I? If it makes them happy, maybe it will help me forget my sorrows."

Johnny and Wa-me-gon-a-biew couldn't believe it. How many times she had lectured them on the evils and dangers of rum and how she had scolded Tau-ga-we-ninne when he had been wounded in the drunken spear-throwing contest. As the day wore on she drank herself into unconsciousness. In the afternoon, the wind switched and began blowing off shore. Most of the Indians were too drunk to travel, but Wa-me-gon-a-biew said to Johnny, "Let us put our mother in the canoe and get her away from here. We can wait on the far shore for the others if we do not find our relatives."

"Good idea," Johnny responded, and they began breaking camp.

"What are you doing?" Mik-e-nuk wanted to know.

Wa-me-gon-a-biew explained, "The wind has changed; we must go while it is calm.

"But it is not calm out there!" Mik-e-nuk pointed. "We are sheltered here, but the east wind is a treacherous wind. A storm is brewing and even now there are whitecaps out on the lake beyond where you can see."

But the boys would not be dissuaded. It just didn't look that bad and they were determined to get their mother away from the drinking and carousing.

Drunk as they were, the other Indians recognized the danger and all but held them back by force.

By the time they reached the middle of the lake the boys knew they were in real trouble. The wind was howling, the waves were vicious, it was beginning to rain, and, worst of all, it was rapidly growing dark. The big drops of water splashing on Net-no-kwa's face revived her; she had pretty well slept off her drunkenness. As she looked around, she asked in bewilderment:

"Where are we?"

"Where are the others?"

"What are we doing out here?"

"Are my sons crazy?"

Her voice increased in volume with each question.

The boys ceased their paddling and tried to explain, but Wa-me-gon-a-biew finally stopped trying to alibi and simply concluded, "We have made a terrible mistake, my mother, we are done for!"

Now totally sober, Net-no-kwa took command, "No, we are not done for! Just paddle and pray!"

With that she grabbed the third paddle and said with a loud voice and in all earnestness, "Kitchi Manitou, forgive my foolishness for getting drunk. Save us from our stupidity!"

She then began a chant of praise.

Johnny, who was in the bow, rested his paddle and looked back at his mother, saying, "It is getting worse." His voice was filled with despair and he was trying hard to choke back the tears of fear.

"No, it is not," Net-no-kwa replied firmly.

"How can you say that, my mother? The waves grow bigger!" Johnny argued.

"That is good—keep paddling," she replied.

Johnny dipped his paddle, but asked in disgust, "Are you still drunk? How can bigger waves be better?"

"They are becoming swells; they are no longer so choppy. Soon it will be just like paddling up and down hill," Net-no-kwa assured him.

And she was right. The canoe became more steady, more easily controlled, but there was a new problem—darkness. The shore had finally come into view but was barely distinguishable during lightning flashes. What they saw was no comfort—ridges and rocks, and lots of them. Soon it was so dark they could see only a few feet in front of the boat. Net-no-kwa resumed her prayer, "Kitchi Manitou—only you can guide us through the rocks and reefs. Without your help we are surely lost."

Just then they passed so close to a rock Johnny cried out in alarm and pushed the canoe away with his paddle. Now it seemed as though there were rocks everywhere.

"Get ready to jump!" Net-no-kwa shouted over the storm.

Suddenly, the mighty crest they were riding threw them—canoe and all—onto a beach! Before the next breaker could hit, all three were out of the canoe and had it pulled up out of danger.

Everyone was soaked, but with the help of some punkwood carried deep in their packs and the ever-reliable flint and steel, a fire was soon roaring back at the storm. When everyone was a little more comfortable and breathing easier, Net-no-kwa picked up where she had left off out on the lake—chastising the boys for starting out across on their own. But Johnny and Wa-me-gon-a-biew were ready this time and launched a counter attack:

"Don't blame us; if you hadn't been drunk, this would not have happened."

"That is right," Johnny chimed in, "We had to save you from yourself."

Then Wa-me-gon-a-biew added the clincher, "If it is all right for you to drink, then I shall drink too. Next time, I shall be the one who gets drunk!"

Johnny echoed, "Me, too."

That did it. Net-no-kwa's mind was suddenly filled with thoughts of how rum had taken her husband from her, and she imagined all sorts of tragedies that might befall her sons if they made good their threat. "I am sorry," she confessed, "It will not happen again. . .but I don't want to hear any more from either of you about drinking!"

And so a truce was declared.

The anxiety and arguing over, Johnny started thinking about how ridiculous Net-no-kwa had looked when she was drunk and started to giggle. His snickering was contagious and soon all three were laughing. About then the rain stopped and sleep came quickly.

As usual, Net-no-kwa was the first one up the next morning—even with her hangover. When Johnny opened his eyes he saw his mother standing on the shore, looking across the lake and shaking her head.

"What is it?" he asked.

"Look for yourself," she replied, "Only the Great Spirit could have guided us through all of those rocks and reefs, and we landed on the only spot of beach I can see anywhere."

When everything had pretty well dried out and the boys had patched a seam in the canoe which had been opened when the vessel was tossed on the shore, the family headed out onto a much quieter Lake Winnipeg. The wind was once again back in the west and by noon the sun had dispersed the last of the clouds. The mouth of the Red River was not reached until well after dark. Here, as expected, they found an Indian village, but not wanting to cause a commotion that time of night, they curled up in their blankets a short distance from the first tent and went to sleep.

The trials of the past few days had taken their toll and the weary travelers were still fast asleep the next morning when several villagers discovered them and awakened them. As they were explaining who they were and where they had come from to the handful who had gathered around, a tall, straightbacked brave approached. Johnny thought he was seeing a ghost! The Indian looked just like Tau-ga-we-ninne!

Suddenly, Net-no-kwa saw the brave and let out a cry of recognition—it was Masqua, Tau-ga-we-ninne's younger brother!

The search was over; the long journey ended.

CHAPTER XI
BUFFALO COUNTRY

Once again Johnny was busy meeting relatives for the first time and making new friends. Since most of the villagers were Ottawa, Net-no-kwa was well known. Even most of those she had never met had heard of her because she was famous for her ability to foresee the future and to direct medicine hunts by means of visions when game was scarce. Word of the death of Tau-ga-we-ninne and Kewatin had preceded the family to the Red River, and the relatives, of course, wanted to hear the details and to express their sympathy.

As a white Indian, Johnny was once again the center of attention. The little children were especially anxious to talk with him and he couldn't help but enjoy being "in the spotlight". On the other hand, Johnny was always a bit fearful that some adult would dislike him because of confrontations they may have had previously with other whites. He had no need for concern in this village, however, and as Net-no-kwa's son, he was as well received as his red brother. Teenagers were also anxious to be his friends, with one exception, his cousin Ka-ka-ge-shig. Johnny wasn't sure just what the problem was. They were the same age and logically should have enjoyed each other's company. But Ka-ka-geshig was forever making some cutting remark, like:

"I never heard of a whiteman yet that was a good hunter," or

"You are 15 years old and have never shot a buffalo?" or

"What a beautiful trophy your blond scalp will make for some Sioux," or

"Skinny braves never make strong warriors."

Although nearly as tall as Johnny, Ka-ka-ge-shig was on the chubby side and Johnny couldn't help but retaliate for this last comment by sneering, "Don't make the mistake of thinking all your fat is muscle!"

From the start, it was obvious that sooner or later the boys would have a showdown, but Johnny was determined to put it off as long as he could, fearful other teenagers would take sides against him. Wa-me-gon-a-biew discouraged his brother further by observing, "Ka-ka-geshig is a good deal heavier than you are, and fat or not, there is no way you are going to beat him."

So Johnny allowed himself to be bullied by his cousin and even when he answered back, was careful not to push his luck too far. It wasn't long before the muscles in his arm were black and blue from Ka-ka-ge-shig's slugging attacks, and he was quickly losing the respect of those who he wanted most to impress.

Meanwhile, Net-no-kwa was having problems of her own. Since she was well known among the Ottawa for her dreams and prophesies, she soon found herself under pressure to demonstrate her powers. Her brother-in-law didn't help matters any; he told story after story of successful medicine hunts at her direction. Of course, Wa-me-gon-a-biew and Johnny had to relate how their mother had saved the Sabaskong village from starvation just the previous winter. Net-no-kwa tried to put off the demands for a demonstration by saying, "I do not like to abuse my gift; I feel it should be saved for times of great need."

Masqua again wasn't very helpful. He pointed out, "This is a time of need, we are nearly out of buffalo meat and you need hides of your own to replace those we have lent you to cover your lodge. Tell us where to hunt them."

Before Net-no-kwa could answer, another brave spoke up, "That would not be a true test; there are so many buffalo in this area. Let her find us a bear!"

Now she was boxed in. Finally she said, "Very well, I shall try. But do not be disappointed if the Great Spirit does not answer my petition just to satisfy your curiosity. But I shall fast and pray and we shall see what happens."

Early the next morning, Net-no-kwa went out from the village to be alone. She was very upset with herself for giving in and feared she would lose credibility as well as embarrass her sons. After wandering rather aimlessly for more than an hour, looking for a comfortable place where she could meditate and pray, Net-no-kwa came across a meadow that had once been flooded by a beaver dam and decided to make her way to the bank of the stream. As she mounted a little hill in the middle of the meadow to get a better view, she almost stepped into a hole at the base of a fallen tree. As it fell, the roots of the tree had been only partially pulled out of the ground, leaving a little cave where they had been. Looking down, Net-no-kwa could scarcely believe her eyes. There, curled up in its den—sound asleep—was a bear. It was only mid-summer; the bear had no business denning up. Her first thought was to wait until the next morning before returning to camp, because there had been no time to fast and the tribe might be suspicious. But by then the bear might awaken and be gone, so she decided to return immediately. "After all," she rationalized, "the Great Spirit must have had mercy on my predicament and led me to this spot."

Back at the village, Net-no-kwa sought out Masqua and asked him to gather the others together. Within minutes a dozen or more had crowded around, urging her to reveal what she had been shown. When Net-no-kwa was satisfied she had an appropriate audience, she proclaimed, "Never has the Great Spirit answered my prayers so swiftly. He has shown me a vision of a large black bear, sleeping in its den. Select a hunter and I shall tell him where to look."

Masqua spoke first, "We all know bears are not in their dens in summer. If it is as Net-no-kwa has said, then surely it is the Great Spirit who has put it there for us and shown it to her."

Before anyone else could volunteer, Johnny cried out, "Let me go! I have never shot a bear."

Net-no-kwa carefully described the trail he must follow and then made Johnny repeat the directions to make sure he would not miss the den. When both were satisfied he could find the place, he ran for his gun and loaded it for bear. Wa-me-gon-a-biew arrived late on the scene and expressed his concern, "I hope that you are right, my mother, and Little Falcon, if our mother is right, you had better not fail or we will all look very foolish!"

Johnny did not answer, but Net-no-kwa was deeply hurt that her son once again would doubt her and responded, "What do you mean '*If* I am right?!' " And she proceeded to chastise him severely. Her sharp tongue was still wagging as Johnny departed at a trot—muzzleloader in hand.

Just out of sight of the village, whom should he meet walking up the trail but Ka-ka-geshig, the last person he wanted to see. The Indian boy stopped in the middle of the path, spread his legs and folded his arms—effectively blocking Johnny's way.

"And where might you go going, *Little* Falcon? Out to hunt Indians?" He asked with a sarcastic snarl.

"No, have you not heard?" Johnny questioned, "My mother has been shown a bear by the Great Spirit and I have been selected to kill it! Now let me pass."

"That is the funniest thing I have ever heard," the Indian boy said with mock laughter. "Why should the Great Spirit show her anything? And if he had, who would be so foolish as to choose you as the hunter? You who have never even killed a bear?"

Johnny could take the personal insult, but challenging his mother was too much. "You father chose me, that's who! Now out of my way or I'll thrash you!" he growled as menacingly as he could sound.

"You lie! Now put down that gun and we'll see who will thrash who!" Ka-ka-geshig challenged.

Johnny did, and the boys came together like a couple of young bull moose. Ka-ka-geshig's heavier weight was a distinct advantage, as he picked Johnny off his feet, dropped him on his back, and came down on top of him with his full weight. Johnny tried to roll him over, but couldn't even come close. Instinctively, he locked his legs in a scissors up around Ka-ka-geshig's ample waist, pulled his chest down against his own with a "bear hug", and then in one motion arched his back and rolled the bigger boy onto his side and then onto his back. Johnny was then able to squeeze his long, sinewy legs and knobby knees into Ka-ka-geshig's back and soft middle. He kept his bear hug but slid his locked wrists up under his opponent's armpit and pulled up with all his might while pushing down with his legs. Ka-ka-geshig cried out in surprise and pain. He twisted and squirmed but Johnny squeezed, and pulled and pushed all the harder, his right knee working deeper and deeper into the pit of the fat boy's stomach. It was all over in minutes as Ka-ka-geshig gasped, "You win!"

But Johnny wouldn't let go. "Tell me you are sorry for what you said about my mother!" He demanded through clenched teeth.

"I'm sorry, I'm sorry!" Ka-ka-geshig assured him.

Johnny eased the pressure but kept his holds. "Now, my cousin, you and I are going to have a little talk! I am sick and tired of you pushing me around and insulting me. Unless there are going to be some changes I'll never let you up!" And he tightened his legs once again to let him know he meant business.

"I had no right to pick on you, all I wanted to do was make you fight. I just wanted to see if I could take you."

"Will it be different now?" Johnny pressed.

"Yes, yes, I promise."

Johnny released his hold with some misgiving; Ka-ka-geshig was lying on one of Johnny's legs and he would have to get up first. But cousin Ka-ka-geshig had enough, and once up, extended his hand and helped Johnny to his feet.

"Little Falcon," Ka-ka-geshig said soberly, "I have made you promises and I will keep them. But I would now ask one of you."

"What is it?" Johnny asked cautiously.

"Promise me you will tell no one of our fight. I have told everyone I could beat you and I will be the laughing stock of our village."

"All right, my cousin, I promise." Johnny said with the smug smile of a victor who could now afford to be merciful.

As the white boy picked up his gun and turned to go, Ka-ka-geshig spoke again, "Little Falcon, if you want—let's be friends."

"Good." Johnny responded, "It shall be so."

As the weeks passed, the boys would experience the magic of hate turned to affection and would wonder a little how a fight could make such good friends. Both kept their word. Johnny never even told Wa-me-gon-a-biew, although he really wanted to brag just a little. When his older brother asked about the turn of events, Johnny simply replied with a knowing smile, "I really can't tell you, but some day I promise to show you."

Wa-me-gon-a-biew just looked at him, grunted, and walked away shaking his head.

Happier than he had been for days, Johnny jogged down the trail. His mother's directions had been clear and he had no problem finding the meadow. Cautiously, he approached the knoll—gun ready. He worked his way up the little hill without a sound. There was the fallen tree, and there was the hole in the ground. With heart pounding, Johnny peered into the darkness. It was still there! With the muzzle just about two feet from the bear's head, he took aim behind the ear, and pulled the trigger. Whoom! The bear never knew what hit him.

Johnny touched the bear's eye with the barrel of his gun. There was no movement. He was dead beyond doubt. As the boy bent down to fasten a tether around the huge, shaggy neck, the bear gave one last dying convulsion! Johnny lurched back, tripped over a log, and landed flat on his back! By the time he had scrambled to his feet he realized how silly he must have looked and was very thankful no one was around to see it—and vowed no one would ever know!

The rope finally in place, Johnny tried to slide the bear up out of the den—but no way, it was huge. No matter. Very proud and very pleased with himself, Johnny ran all the way back to the village. He lifted the flap over the lodge door and caught Net-no-kwa pacing nervously back and forth within the confines of the shelter.

"I got him!" he announced with a big grin. Net-no-kwa embraced her son with a bear hug that rivaled the one he had clamped on Ka-ka-geshig earlier in the afternoon. Then, with tears of joy and pride flowing down her cheeks, she reached up and pulled her son's face down next to hers and nearly suffocated him with kisses.

Together, they sought out Masqua and announced their triumph as nonchalantly as if there were never a doubt from the beginning. People began gathering around, almost in awe. Johnny spotted Ka-ka-geshig standing on the edge of the crowd and when he caught his eye gave him a wink. He was more than pleased when his cousin winked back and smiled. Wa-me-gon-a-biew saw the commotion but stayed clear, not sure what his mother might say. Later, however, when Masqua asked for volunteers to bring back the bear, he quickly offered to help—even though it was considered "squaw's work"—hoping to redeem himself in the eyes of his mother.

The next day, the family celebrated the Feast of First Fruits in Johnny's honor and the whole village was invited.

Wa-me-gon-a-biew had been pretty quiet, but when he caught his brother alone, he teased, "The bear really wasn't alive when you found it, was it? How long do you think it had been dead?"

Laughing, he let Johnny throw him to the ground and win his second wrestling match in two days.

It was not too long after the celebration, that Masqua stopped at the family's lodge one evening and announced, "Tomorrow, I and my son, Ka-ka-geshig, will be going buffalo hunting. Since you will be needing hides to replace those loaned to you and since you probably could use some meat, perhaps you boys would like to join us?"

Before his first sentence was finished, the brothers were on their feet in anticipation, and when he had finished his invitation, they responded almost in unison, "Yes, we would like that."

"Have you ever ridden horses?" Masqua asked.

"Many times—even bare back!" Johnny replied.

For once Johnny could do something the older brother could not, and Wa-me-gon-a-biew reluctantly replied, "I have never had such an opportunity."

Johnny looked up at his uncle and asked "May I teach him?" Wa-me-gon-a-biew began a protest, but Masqua cut him off as he said, "I think that would be a good idea." He turned to his son who had walked up during the conversation and directed, "Ka-ka-ge-shig, fetch your horse, and you can help Little Falcon teach your cousin how to ride."

Wa-me-gon-a-biew was stuck and he knew it. By nightfall he had learned how to handle the pony fairly well but with little real help from his brother and cousin who thoroughly enjoyed the older boy's lack of experience and humiliating mistakes—particularly when he slid off the animal's back and lit flat on his own!

The hunters were off before daybreak; the boys riding horses borrowed from generous neighbors. Johnny was impressed with the flat, open prairies. He had never seen anything like it in all of his travels.

The first buffalo were sighted late in the morning—a small herd of eleven animals. Two of them were huge bulls, and although not quite as big as moose, they looked larger on the open terrain.

"Ka-ka-geshig," Masqua directed, "that last animal appears to be a dry cow without a calf. It should be good eating. Take it. Show your cousins how it is done."

Ka-ka-geshig needed no further encouragement. He was off at full gallop, catching the animals completely by surprise. He was only a few yards from the cow as he swung by, discharging his muzzleloader at point blank range into the neck, making a quick clean kill, and the buffalo went down in a heap.

Johnny and Wa-me-gon-a-biew were a little concerned as the rest of the animals took off at full speed. Masqua detected their anxiety and reassured them, "Do not worry. We will catch them. When we do, each of you take one of the big herd bulls. They will make fine robes. I will go last and shoot one of the others."

With that, the three were off, Ka-ka-geshig staying behind to work on his cow. The buffalo had disappeared into a coulee, but when the hunters came over a rise of ground and looked down into the draw, they saw the herd had already stopped running. Wa-me-gon-a-biew was still unsure of his horse, but by the time the animals were aware of the hunters and tried to scramble up the hill, Johnny was alongside the biggest bull and dropped him with a shot through the chest cavity. The huge beast plowed the earth like a bulldozer as he went down.

Meanwhile, Wa-me-gon-a-biew was having his problems. He was afraid to ride at top speed and was never quite in full control of his pony, and the horse knew it. The chase lasted for more than a mile before Wa-me-gon-a-biew closed in near enough for a sure shot. He also placed his ball in the chest cavity, but the big bull roared on for at least 200 yards farther before collapsing.

Masqua waited patiently for Wa-me-gon-a-biew to score and then dropped a yearling for more good eating.

Once butchered, the meat was wrapped in the hides and then lashed to skid poles and trailed behind the horses back to camp—arriving well after dark.

Still later, as the two bone-tired but very happy teenagers rolled up in their blankets, Johnny just couldn't resist asking, "Wa-me-gon-a-biew, are you asleep?"

"No, but I would like to be!" was the reply.

"Well, I was just wondering if you realized I shot my buffalo before you shot yours? I finally got a first of a kind before you did. And I didn't have to wait until I was almost 19 to shoot a buffalo—or to learn how to ride a horse!"

Silence.

All Johnny could hear was the heavy breathing of his brother feigning sleep. He hated being ignored but he figured he had made his point and left well enough alone.

CHAPTER XII
WA-ME-GON-A-BIEW GOES ON THE WARPATH

With the first signs of autumn, the village leadership spoke of moving to a better hunting ground for food and furs. A council was held and it was decided to go up Red River to the Assinneboine, and then up that stream to a place called "Prairie Portage". Masqua used the occasion to call the attention of the leadership to the plight of his relatives. In their behalf, he urged, "These young men are without a father. It is our duty to teach them how to be good hunters and trappers. Until they learn, we must share the fruits of our endeavors with the family."

As Masqua expected, the chief and the members of the council agreed without hesitation. It was the custom.

It was also agreed in council that a favorite trader, known as "Pierre", would be contacted and invited to go with them. Pierre worked out of old Fort Maurepas and had been in the habit of operating a winter post with these villagers for several years. The arrangement was mutually advantageous: the trader would have a monopoly on the furs harvested and the Indians would be given credit for their immediate needs against those furs. So Pierre was not surprised when the offer was made, and the tribe was not surprised when Pierre accepted.

It did not take the villagers long to collapse their lodges and prepare for departure. Most goods were transported by canoe. Since birchbark was not plentiful in the area, several of the crafts were covered instead with the skins of moose and elk. The remainder of the tribe moved along shore on horseback, trailing family possessions behind on pole skids. The journey up the Red River was not difficult. The once boisterous currents of spring and early summer had become lazy, making paddling relatively easy.

The Assinneboin proved to be quite a different stream. It was more windy than the Red and had a gravel bottom, making the water more clear. The place called Prairie Portage was reached without mishap. Those on horseback arrived first, having taken several shortcuts cross-country rather than follow the serpent-like curves of the Assinneboine. The planned campsite was about 70 miles by land from the Red River, but much more than that by canoe.

Net-no-kwa and the boys traveled the water route and had quite a surprise awaiting them when they arrived at Prairie Portage. It was in the form of four Ottawa braves from the old village near Lake Huron. These men had encountered those villagers who had been traveling by horseback and had learned that Net-no-kwa and her family would soon be arriving via the river. The leader of the group was Pe-shau-ba, an Ottawa war chief and a brother-in-law through Net-no-kwa's first marriage. The other three were called "his young men" and were named Waus-so (the lightning), Sa-wing-wa (he that stretches his wings), and Say-git-to (he that scares all men). While Pe-shau-ba told of news from the village and listened in turn to Net-no-kwa's tale of sorrows, Johnny stared at the awesome features of the big man. Possibly handsome at one time, his face was distorted by the scars of many battles. Worst of all, the end of the chief's nose and the lobe of his right ear had been bitten off in the rough and tumble of close combat. The left ear was pierced and from it hung a heavy brass ring which over the years had pulled the lobe out of shape.

By and by Pe-shau-ba noticed Johnny's stare and remarked, "You think I am ugly, no?"

Johnny felt as though he had been caught stealing and protested in embarrassment, "No - no - no!"

"Well, let me tell you, my son, I earned each of these scars the hard way—and on each hangs a tale that would make the hair raise on the top of your head! Furthermore, most of the braves who gave them to me are no longer among the living. My war bonnet displays thirty-nine feathers: one for each scalp I have taken. But let me show you my most recent scar—still red with infection!"

With that, Pe-shau-ba dropped his blanket from his shoulder, revealing an ugly arrow wound high on his right side.

"But not to worry," the old brave went on, "It cost a Sioux his life."

Realizing that he had shaken Johnny's composure, Pe-shau-ba placed his big hand on the boy's shoulder, smiled broadly and said, "Never mind, just as others have taught you the ways of the hunter and trap-

Pe-shau-ba: His face was distorted by the scars of many battles. Worst of all, the end of the chief's nose and the lobe of his right ear had been bitten off in the rough and tumble of close combat.

per, I will teach you and Wa-me-gon-a-biew the ways of the warrior."

Net-no-kwa winced noticeably and changed the subject, "So tell me, Pe-shau-ba, what brings you and your young men way out here?"

"We have left our village and families behind for the same reasons you and Tau-ga-we-ninne journeyed west," He replied. "We are seeking better hunting grounds and eventually may return for the others. But while we are here, we are enjoying the excitement of once again being on the warpath. There is no one left to fight back home—except the Long Knives. And," he added slowly and deliberately after a pause during which he looked straight at Johnny, "that seems to be a losing cause."

"Meanwhile, Net-no-kwa," He went on, "Why not join our forces? We will help your sons with hunting and trapping and you can sew and mend our clothing and prepare our food."

"I think that would be good." Net-no-kwa replied politely. But in her heart she was more than a little concerned about the old warrior's influence on her Wa-me-gon-a-biew and Little Falcon.

Before long, the snows of winter descended on the new village in the wrath of a prairie blizzard. Game, so abundant a few days before, seemed to be swallowed up in the drifts. Although the hunters returned with a buffalo or elk almost daily for food, trapping was alarmingly nonproductive. After a few weeks of frustration and disappointment, a council was held with trader Pierre and it was decided it would be wise to move the camp to Clearwater Lake where there would be more shelter from the severe winter for both the hunter and the hunted.

Travel proved to be extremely difficult. Canoes were of no value on frozen streams and there were not nearly enough horses to accommodate all the villagers. It was hard work all the way. The only part of the journey Johnny enjoyed was the day when he, Wa-me-gon-a-biew, and Ka-ka-ge-shig were included in a hunting party which forged ahead on their snowshoes in search of game. About midday, three elk were spotted just as they were disappearing down a draw. The boys were able to run faster than the men and reached the little valley well ahead of the rest of the party. They spotted the majestic animals—all three antlered bulls—bucking the drifts of chest-deep snow as they worked their way up a little hill at the end of the coulee. In minutes they were in easy range—something that would have been impossible any other time of year. Each boy took an animal in the order in which they stood. Johnny and Wa-me-gon-a-biew both made clean kills, but the overweight Ka-ka-ge-shig was huffing and puffing from the exertion and his wavering gun barrel caused a miss. The brothers completed reloading first, but gallantly restrained themselves from shooting, allowing their cousin to redeem himself with a second shot. While waiting for the other hunters to catch up, Johnny and Wa-me-gon-a-biew had just enough time to tease Ka-ka-ge-shig about his physical condition—and were promptly rewarded with a mitfull of snow in the face!

These were the first elk either of the brothers had taken, and when the wintry caravan called a halt that night, Net-no-kwa proclaimed the Feast of First Fruits would be observed as the evening meal.

All things—both good and bad—must come to an end, one way or another, and the treacherous journey through the drifted snow was finally completed with the arrival at Clearwater Lake. Just as the leadership of the tribe had predicted, the somewhat improved shelter made hunting and trapping much easier—and there was less snowfall besides. Traplines were established and the camp was soon busy piling up furs—mostly beaver and martin. Johnny and Wa-me-gon-a-biew teamed up with Pe-shau-ba, as planned, and they never tired of his endless stories of war parties on the attack or of defending against the Sioux. The old warrior, in turn, enjoyed his eager audience. One night as the three sat at a shelter a day's journey from the new village, and as the campfire worked its magic and loosened men's tongues, the boys pressed Pe-shau-ba, "When do you think you will again join a war party?"

"Perhaps this spring," was the reply. "The Mandans have asked for help against the Minnetarees. They are forever attacking their village."

"Who are 'the Mandans'?" Johnny asked.

"They are quite a different people," Pe-shau-ba responded. "They stay in one place in a permanent village. Their earthen homes are protected by a stockade and waterways. At one time all tribes preyed on them—perhaps because they are so different. Over the years, however, we have learned they are a good people—peace loving—and the Ojibway, Ottawa and Cree now help them fight their battles."

At this point, Wa-ma-gon-a-biew drew closer to old Pe-shau-ba, looked him straight in the eye, and said, "Dear friend, when you go in the spring, take me with you. I have seen 18 summers; I am a man. It is not right that I have never seen battle."

"Me, too," Johnny interrupted, "I - - -"

But Pe-shau-ba cut off the white boy's attempt to speak. "No, Little Falcon, you are too young, and your mother would never permit it. As for you, Wa-me-gon-a-biew, we shall see. I shall speak with Net-no-kwa when the time is right." Then turning back to Johnny he added, "On the other hand, Little Falcon, I shall be instructing your brother in the arts of war, and you may as well join in those studies in preparation for that day when you will be old enough."

This assurance only partially satisfied Johnny's appetite for adventure, and he promised himself he would work on his mother and beg and plead if need be until she gave in.

Pe-shau-ba was as good as his word. Frequently, during the hunting and trapping expeditions which followed that winter, he would point out such strategies as the importance of camouflage as illustrated by the grouse, the value of remaining perfectly still so as to be undetected as with the deer, the importance of the hunter—or warrior—never showing his profile against the horizon and many other suggestions, any one of which could save a brave's life. Battle plans were discussed many a night around the campfire and included such lessons as the advantage of surprise attack, the value of a pincers movement by charging on two fronts, the deception of drawing an enemy into a trap, the techniques of diverting attention from the main thrust, and the wisdom of retreating when the cause was hopeless.

Pe-shau-ba also told of the many traditions and superstitions observed by braves as they went to war. It was customary, for example, for each warrior to sleep every night with his face towards home. Young braves on the warpath for the first time blackened their faces and upper bodies with charcoal. Each brave used his own blanket; it was bad luck to share a blanket with anyone while on the warpath. No one ever sat on the bare ground while out on a campaign nor would he allow his feet to get wet. If it was absolutely necessary to travel across a swamp or stream, special medicines were administered to the legs and feet to "neutralize" the bad luck. It was also considered an ill omen to step over anyone else's property—such as a knife or article of clothing. Should this inadvertently happen, the transgressor was obliged to let the property owner throw him to the ground as hard as he wished—to break the spell. Each carried his own drinking bowl and it was proper to drink from one side on the journey out and the other side on the return. These bowls were left hanging in a tree on the last day before reaching the home village, or if no tree was around, they were discarded on the prairie.

When the war party lay down to sleep at night, sticks were poked into the ground all around the men, forming a symbolic enclosure, with an opening on the end facing the enemy. The braves lay down in rank order, with the chief by the opening and the black-faced beginners at the opposite end. Many carried with them possessions which had belonged to dead friends or to children who had died. These were called "je-be-ug" and were thrown on the field of battle to enhance the reward the departed would receive in the life hereafter.

This latter practice prompted Wa-me-gon-a-biew to ask, "What else determines a warrior's reward in the life hereafter?"

"Well," Pe-shau-ba sucked on his pipe, "How bravely he fights and how good a man he is in general. But if he is scalped, he will be without hair in the after-life and will not have as great recognition."

"I think I have a pretty good idea what the good place is like," Johnny said, "but what is it like where the bad people go?"

"Life there is very difficult," the old chief replied. "It is a place where you are very hungry and you can see thousands of trout through six feet of clear ice, and there is no way you can get at them. Or you are hunting a deer and a big buck is forever disappearing over the horizon as you climb each hill, or you are very cold and all the wood around you is wet and you have no dry tinder—as you try again and again to start a fire with your numb fingers."

The boys stared at each other in silence.

Pe-shau-ba went on, "Speaking of spiritual things, I have often sought the guidance of the Great Spirit when going into battle, and that is true of most chiefs I know. One way we do this is to have the youngest warriors clear away the sod and all growth from a small patch of soil and scrape out a smooth surface. Then I sit down facing this little clearing and place sticks in the soil forming an enclosure, but leaving the far end—towards the enemy—open. I then place two smooth stones which I carry with me on the warpath, on the soil at my end of the enclosure. As I pray and concentrate I move these stones without thinking towards the open end. Then I summon the more experienced warriors and together we study the paths of the stones and try to determine what strategy the Great Spirit has shown us as we plan our attack."

All of which made Wa-me-gon-a-biew all the more eager to go on the warpath and Johnny all the more envious of his brother and all the more determined to find a way to be included.

When Net-no-kwa finally learned from Pe-shau-ba of his intent to take her oldest son with him on the warpath, she was most distraught and scolded him with a tongue lashing that finally drove him from the lodge. "I have lost two husbands and two sons. Would you now take another loved one from me?"

But eventually Wa-me-gon-a-biew's pleadings prevailed and Net-no-kwa reluctantly accepted the whole matter as inevitable. Johnny, meanwhile, knew better than to say anything at the time but as the first warm days of spring arrived, he decided he would have to make his move before it was too late and broached the subject one day when his mother appeared to be in a particularly good mood. Her reaction, however, was so emotional that he left the lodge in the knowledge his only hope was to sneak away with the war party.

A few weeks later, a messenger arrived on horseback from the Mandan village and threw down a deerskin glove by the council fire—the symbol of a call for armed help. A score of volunteers quickly responded and departure was scheduled for the very next morning. As a greenhorn warrior, Wa-me-gon-a-biew was instructed to blacken his face and upper body and to walk in the footsteps of the experienced warriors whenever there was an opportunity. That evening preparations were made at a rapid pace. Pemican and jerky were provided by the women, knives were sharpened, bows and arrows examined, bullets molded, and muzzle loaders checked for accuracy. Since the trapping season was over, it was agreed the war party on its return would meet the villagers at Lake Winnipeg where the Red River flows into the lake. Pe-shau-ba told Net-no-kwa, "I will expect a full kettle and a keg of rum waiting for me!"

Johnny made one last plea to his mother, pointing out, "I will be 16 in a few days. I am even taller than my brother, and the sooner I learn the art of fighting the better I will become and the better my chances to live to an old age - - -."

He paused to catch his breath and that was the last chance he had to say a word! In frustration, he resolved to tag along at a distance behind the war party as it left the next day.

Thus it was not yet daybreak when Johnny reached for his gun in the darkness of the lodge as he prepared to sneak out. But it was not there! A quiet but frantic search convinced him that his mother had hidden the muzzleloader. Heartsick and angry he slipped into the false dawn of early morning.

Johnny hid himself near the horse pen. Believing there would possibly be a spare muzzleloader or at least a hand gun he could borrow from someone in the war party, he was still determined to follow along. When it was light enough to see, the warriors began to assemble. The crisp morning air was filled with the sound of their activity and the voices of the braves were tense in a mood of excitement and anticipation. Friends and family also began arriving to see them off and wish them well. From his hiding place, Johnny was easily able to pick out his brother by his blackened face and body. Within the hour, final preparations were completed and the procession moved out. Some were on horseback, but most followed on foot. The white boy's heart ached as he watched Wa-me-gon-a-biew take his place at the end of the line—carefully stepping in the footsteps of old Pe-shau-ba. He thought, "I'd give anything to be following in my brother's footsteps!"

When the party was out of sight and the last of the village people who had come to see them off had returned to their lodges, Johnny came out of hiding. His face grim with determination, he stole a quick glance at the village to be sure no one was watching, and then jogged off in the direction the war party had taken. All he carried were the remains of the charcoal Wa-me-gon-a-biew had used to blacken his body. In that one quick glance he had not noticed his mother, anxiously peering from behind the nearest lodge. Little did he know that she had suspected he might do this and had alerted Pe-shau-ba, making him promise to send her son back.

Johnny had no trouble over-taking the war party and stayed just out of sight until they made camp for the night. It was then that he took out the charcoal and rubbed his face and upper body until they were quite black. With pounding heart he walked slowly towards the encampment. Pe-shau-ba had been expecting Johnny, and when he saw him, quickly walked out to meet him. Before the white boy could speak, and he really didn't know what to say anyway—the veteran began to scold, "Shaw-shaw-wa-be-na-see, I am most disappointed that you would disobey your mother and sneak after us like a coyote! A true warrior obeys those who are in authority. A true warrior has patience, lest he make a foolish move at an inopportune time. You are clearly not ready to be a warrior. Now return at once to the village or I shall thrash you until you cannot walk!"

Johnny was overwhelmed. He had not anticipated so violent a response. Without a word he turned his back, bowed his head, and began his slow return. Old Pe-shau-ba was touched. "Wait, my son," he called, "Your obedience to my command is your first step on the journey to becoming a warrior. But you know you must help your mother; it was wrong to leave her alone without making arrangements for her care. Now go to her and help her on the journey to the Lake of Dirty Water. I will see you there and promise to do my best to persuade her to let you go next time."

Johnny still couldn't find words to utter, but finally managed a weak smile and nodded his head in agreement before once again turning his face towards home. Only an hour or so of daylight remained, but it was enough for Johnny to reach a small stream where he used some sand to scrub off the charcoal before curling up in the tall grass for the night.

The next day, half starved, he jogged most of the way back to the village. Net-no-kwa scarcely looked up as Johnny entered the lodge. She didn't even acknowledge that he had been gone. He noticed his muzzleloader back in its usual place but made no comment. Net-no-kwa finally broke the silence by saying, "There is some food left in the kettle; put it over the coals and finish it up."

Johnny was surprised to find a huge elk roast; he ate all of it.

A few day later, Net-no-kwa told Johnny, "I would like to begin our journey to the Lake of Dirty Water. I want to be there when Wa-me-gon-a-biew, Pe-shau-ba and the others arrive. It is apparent the rest of the village is in no hurry to depart, so perhaps you would like to invite Ka-ka-ge-shig to join us and go on ahead."

Bored without Wa-me-gon-a-biew around and still upset with having been left behind and then making a fool of himself, Johnny lost no time seeking out his cousin and extending the invitation. Meanwhile, Net-no-kwa arranged with Pierre for full credit for the furs taken during the winter.

Thus is was that two days later, Net-no-kwa and the two teenagers headed down the Assinneboin in the direction of the Red River. The weather was ideal, the current gentle, and all went well until the afternoon of the second day—when a cloud of dust on the horizon indicated that a sizeable party of men on horseback was headed in their direction. Net-no-kwa paused with her paddle in mid-air and said with concern, "There is no way of knowing if they are friends or enemies by the dust they make. We had better hide in the bushes in that draw up ahead until they pass or until we see who they are."

The canoe was no sooner concealed than a band of thirty or more painted warriors on horseback came into view. They reached the river only a few rods from where the trio lay hidden, and then swung east along the bank. Johnny knew from the alarm he read in his mother's eyes that they were Sioux. When the last Indian and horse were out of sight, Net-no-kwa confirmed Johnny's fears and then went on, "We best remain here until dark, and then travel only at night from now on until we reach the Lake of Dirty Water."

Johnny and Ka-ka-ge-shig nodded their assent. Sometime later, when all had regained their composure. The Indian boy teased, "Little Falcon, I thought you wanted to fight the Sioux—why did you not attack?"

"Had there been twenty or less I would have wiped them out, but there were a few too many for me to guarantee the safety of you and my mother!" was Johnny's smart reply.

The moon disappeared early that night and the travelers were grateful for the protection the darkness had to offer. But as they moved downstream, every strange sound filled their hearts with panic and they would then rest their paddles in total silence until they had drifted well past the possible danger. The third night, as they reached the mouth of the Assinneboin, was a little too exciting. Again, there was no moon, but the stars in a cloudless sky made it possible to see better than anyone wanted to. Just as they were entering the larger river, an owl hooted on the south bank of the Assinneboin. Immediately another answered on the opposite bank—and then a third cried out across the river.

"It is the Sioux!" Net-no-kwa whispered. "We are discovered. Let us try to paddle back up the Assinneboin!"

Johnny was in the bow and stared ahead anxiously into the darkness. Suddenly, he saw a movement on the water ahead. He turned and whispered hoarsely, "Someone is swimming towards us to upset our canoe!"

Net-no-kwa promptly replied, "Take the sturgeon harpoon and kill him! There is no choice!"

Ka-ka-ge-shig handed him the spear. Johnny took it with trembling hands and laid the handle on his shoulder in the ready position as the canoe closed in. Later he would remember thinking, "It isn't hard to kill someone when it is your life or theirs." Only a few feet to go. . .he cocked his arm. . .but just then the object exploded across the surface in the form of a goose and her brood of young ones!

At the moment, no one laughed. The situation remained far too serious, but a few hours later when they were nestled safely in the cover they had used the previous day, Ka-ka-ge-shig had a few choice things to say to his cousin!

It was decided it would be best to remain in hiding until the villagers caught up. Meanwhile, the boys hunted with bows and arrows so as not to reveal their presence. Small, well hidden fires were used for cooking at daybreak and dusk when the smoke could not be detected. So there was genuine rejoicing a few days later when a flotilla of canoes coming downstream was identified as their friends.

Scouts were sent ahead. They returned with good news that no Sioux were to be found. There were signs of a recent encampment at the junction of the two rivers, but no one would ever know for sure whether the Sioux had indeed been there that night or if there actually had been three owls that had caused the canoe to turn back.

At Lake Winnipeg, they found Wa-me-gon-a-biew, Pe-shau-ba and the others already on hand. Johnny made a bee-line for his brother and demanded to hear all about the battle. But Wa-me-gon-a-biew replied with dejection, "There was no battle. The Sioux had been driven off by others before we got there and the Mandans were no longer in need of help. We stayed around for awhile to make sure the Sioux would not come back, but then the tribes that came to help started arguing and fighting among themselves so Pe-shau-ba and Masqua decided it was time to leave."

"Well then," Johnny said boastfully, "Let me tell you about some real excitement and how close we were to a big Sioux war party!"

Wa-me-gon-a-biew listened in envy as his younger brother described every little detail of the near encounter. But somehow, when Johnny told about the incident involving the three owls in the night, he just happened to forget about the goose and her brood. Unfortunately, Ka-ka-ge-shig came walking up during the story telling and asked Johnny, "Didn't you forget the most exciting moment of all?"

"I don't think so," was the weak and somewhat cool reply.

"Then I will refresh your memory," Ka-ka-ge-shig offered, and he proceeded to relate how Johnny couldn't tell a warrior from a goose.

"Really," Johnny broke in with a touch of indignation, "I didn't think the incident was worth talking about."

With that, he turned his back and walked away—blushing—as Wa-me-gon-a-biew and Ka-ka-ge-shig doubled over with laughter.

CHAPTER XIII
LOVE COMES TO WA-ME-GON-A-BIEW

The stay at the mouth of the Red River was not to be a long one. Pe-shau-ba was growing anxious to return for his family at Lake Huron and Net-no-kwa thought it would be a good opportunity to travel along as far as the village at Rainy River so that she might visit her daughter, Win-et-ka, and her family. The idea of returning to the beautiful tall timber country and once again hunting and trapping with Maji-go-bo, his young brother-in-law, excited Johnny and he asked Wa-me-gon-a-biew, "Are you ready for a change of scenery?"

"Not really," was his brother's surprising reply.

"Would you rather stay here on this lake that is so big it is dangerous to travel on, and when you turn around and look all you see is sky and prairie?" Johnny pressed.

Wa-me-gon-a-biew only shrugged. What Johnny didn't understand was that at 19 years of age his brother was not only feeling a desire for independence but had taken notice of a girl a little younger than he—the daughter of the chief himself, old Ce-naw-wick-un (he that produces a rattling sound as he moves his body). The truth of the matter dawned on Johnny the next day when he found his brother whittling a flute from a piece of ash limb and, later that day, found him playing that flute near the lodge where No-din-ens was helping her mother with the evening meal.

That night as the brothers lay down to sleep, Johnny poked Wa-me-gon-a-biew in the ribs and whispered, "I heard the funniest noise this afternoon. I thought at first it was music, but it was such a squeaky sound it couldn't have been that. It came from over by Chief Ce-naw-wick-un's lodge. Maybe it was just someone learning to whistle - - -."

At this point, the heavy arm of Wa-me-gon-a-biew came down across Johnny's mid-section, evoking a loud, "Ooff!"

It was some time before Johnny regained his breath, but when he did he began to snort and snicker; he knew he had gotten under his brother's skin. Not content to leave well enough alone, he continued, "If you were trying to impress No-din-ens, I'm sure you did," and then after a long pause, "But I won't say how!"

Johnny waited for the blows to fall—but nothing came. Wa-me-gon-a-biew was more embarrassed than angry; he didn't know quite what to say or do. This wasn't the response Johnny wanted or expected and it bothered him. After a pause that was so long it became awkward, the white youth reached out until his hand rested on his Red brother's arm and said, "I think she's pretty, too."

Wa-me-gon-a-biew responded with a grunt that spoke his appreciation for Johnny's backing off, and both boys rolled over on their sides and went to sleep.

Net-no-kwa couldn't help but overhear the whispered conversation, and the next day she took Wa-me-gon-a-biew aside and assured him, "My son, I understand your interest in No-din-ens. You are at an age when you should start thinking about taking a wife. I am not anxious to see you leave our lodge, but when you are ready, whether it is No-din-ens or someone else, you may be sure I will be willing to speak to the parents in your behalf."

Wa-me-gon-a-biew was almost overcome with relief. All his anxieties about approaching his mother had been needless. But still embarrassed to talk about such matters, he finally stammered, "I—I thank you."

Net-no-kwa turned to go about her business when the youth reached out and lightly touched her shoulder. "My mother," he blurted out, "I am sure No-din-ens is the one." Then, before Net-no-kwa could say anything, he quickly added, "Will you speak to Chief Ce-naw-wick-un?"

Thoughts tumbled through the mother's head. She really wasn't ready to give up her son—but, after all, he was of age. If she asked the chief and he said "Yes," then she couldn't very well back off. "But he is such an important man," she reasoned, "And No-din-ens is a beautiful girl. Surely the parents would want someone more important for a son-in-law—someone older, a proven warrior and hunter."

Feeling assured that the family would say, "No," Net-no-kwa nodded her assent, and then added, "I will speak to No-din-ens' parents today or tomorrow."

Wa-me-gon-a-biew let out a warwhoop and took off on the run.

Johnny had watched from out of ear-shot, but guessed the nature of the conversation and wondered if he would ever behave so foolishly.

And so it was that after the evening meal Net-no-kwa made her way to the chief's lodge. As she drew closer her heart was filled with mixed emotions. On the one hand she hoped he would reject the offer; on the other hand her pride told her Wa-me-gon-a-biew was good enough for any maid in the village. In the end, pride won out, and when Chief Ce-naw-wick-un took note of Net-no-kwa's presence she began the conversation with the words, "I bring you good news."

"And what is that?" Ce-naw-wick-un asked.

"My oldest son, Wa-me-gon-a-biew, has it in his heart that he would take your daughter, No-din-ens, as his wife." Then added quickly, "He is a fine young man—strong, a good hunter and trapper—and a good provider. . ."

The chief was obviously surprised and found it hard to reply, but finally stammered, "Your son's interest in our daughter is—a —flattering, but her mother and I will have to talk about this." Then, regaining his composure, added, "If we agree, No-din-ens will come to your lodge tomorrow at sundown. If she does not come, you will know we feel it would not work out."

Net-no-kwa knew it would be improper to press the issue further, so she thanked the chief for his consideration and quietly slipped away.

Wa-me-gon-a-biew hugged his mother when she told him she had fulfilled her promise and danced her around and around in his excitement.

"Don't assume too much, my son," Net-no-kwa cautioned, "Chief Ce-naw-wick-un wasn't very encouraging."

"But I just know he will say 'yes.' He has to!" the youth exclaimed and he even gave Johnny a bear hug.

Wa-me-gon-a-biew didn't sleep a wink that night and was restless all the next day. Johnny wasn't so sure he liked the whole idea. It just wouldn't be the same with his brother married—but he said nothing. As the long day finally neared its end, the family entered the lodge to wait—as was the custom. Johnny and Wa-me-gon-a-biew sat on either side of the entry and Net-no-kwa took her place opposite the doorway. The lodge grew darker as the sun sank below the horizon. Hardly a word was spoken as the family waited—staring at each other. Tension and anxiety filled the air. Minutes seemed like hours and Wa-me-gon-a-biew's concern turned to anxiety and anxiety to despondency. As he opened his mouth to speak his disappointment, lovely little No-din-ens stepped into the lodge, not having made a sound as she approached. She looked first at Johnny and the white youth's heart jumped into his throat, "What if she thinks I am the one?" he asked himself.

If she had been confused, the alarm she read in Johnny's eyes would have told her he was surely not her husband to be—so she smiled her amusement, nodded, and then turned towards her suitor and gracefully sat down at his side, thus signifying that her family had accepted the proposal. Poor Wa-me-gon-a-biew was beside himself—but speechless! Only Net-no-kwa's poise and easy manner saved the awkward situation.

The next day, Net-no-kwa completed her obligation by negotiating gifts of hides, furs and rum. A great feast was held that evening to solemnize the marriage.

It was only a few days later when the young couple faced their first serious problem. Wa-me-gon-a-biew wanted to join his family and relatives on their trip to Rainy Lake, but No-din-ens was reluctant to leave her family and friends. A compromise was finally worked out: they would stay with the Red River band until the next spring and then journey to Rainy Lake. All of which made Net-no-kwa a little uneasy—with only her younger son left to help her once Pe-shau-ba continued on to Lake Huron. She was also concerned about Wa-me-gon-a-biew and No-din-ens traveling by themselves. It was Masqua who came forth with a solution. He announced, "I would like to see Lake of the Woods and Rainy Lake once again—but not until one more season of trapping, so take my son, Ka-ka-geshig, with you and we will come east next spring with Wa-me-gon-a-biew and No-din-ens."

Net-no-kwa was satisfied; Johnny was delighted.

Shortly thereafter, preparations were made for the departure. Johnny really felt strange saying "goodbye" to his brother. They had been so close; he feared it would never again be quite the same. He and Wa-me-gon-a-biew had seldom talked seriously—but this time it was different. "Are you certain you will join us in the spring?" he pressed.

Wa-me-gon-a-biew put a hand on each of his brother's shoulders, looked him in the eye and solemnly pledged, "I promise."

Only then did the usually light-hearted Johnny smile and ask, "How does it feel to have to look up to your younger brother?"

Wa-me-gon-a-biew gave him a playful shove and snorted, "Don't let it worry you—I can still handle my *younger* brother!"

Maybe, yes. . .maybe, no—but when you see me in the spring I will be too big for you to push around!" was Johnny's reply.

A wrestling match was the inevitable result of such conversation—but his time it took Wa-me-gon-a-biew a good 15 minutes or more to make his white brother say "Uncle".

"See?" Johnny panted from underneath, "You have just won your last match with me!"

"That's big talk from the one on the bottom—*Little* Falcon! I look forward more than you know to putting you in your place next spring!" And with that, he let him up.

Pe-shau-ba chose an entirely different route for the trip back east. Instead of crossing big Lake Winnipeg, he led his small band up the Red River, then across to Roseau Lake, up the Cow Parsley River, then across several miles of swampy muskeg, and finally down the Reed River to Buffalo Bay of Lake of the Woods. Without a doubt, it was a good short cut.

Johnny, Net-no-kwa and Ka-ka-ge-shig traveled together in one canoe. Johnny was grateful for his cousin's companionship—it made it easier leaving his brother behind. They had become very good friends since their initial conflict.

Because the Sioux had been seen so recently in the area, the canoeists traveled by night and slept by day—under cover—until they reached Little Roseau Lake. This was Ojibway country so thereafter they felt safe. Next came the swampy portages, well worn by generations and generations of moccasins.

It was a beautiful, calm day when the party reached the Lake of the Woods. On the way to the mouth of the Rainy River, Pe-shau-ba chose to take a considerable detour north into the islands. He had this area in mind as the future home for his family and followers. Johnny had never given serious thought to settling in any one place, but as they moved through the heavily wooded islands and saw an abundance of big game as well as many beaver houses and heavy popple cutting—indicating an abundance of this favorite fur-bearing animal—he suggested to Ka-ka-geshig, "What do you say we encourage our own families to settle here?"

The Indian youth rested his paddle as though engaged in deep thought before replying, and then answered, "Yes, that would be good. The islands give shelter from stormy winds; one could always get out to hunt or fish. There is no shortage of fuel to keep the lodges warm in the winter, and there are many big birch trees to provide bark for canoes and for shelter."

"Not only that," Johnny added, "but waterways from this lake lead in all directions: north, south, east and west. It would be a good base from which to travel."

Net-no-kwa caught the spirit of the conversation and added, "There are several trading posts on the lake, nor would it be too difficult to travel to Grand Portage or even Mackinac to get top market for furs." She then reinforced her position by adding, "And it wouldn't be too far from Win-et-ka's family either."

When the band stopped to camp over-night on little Center Island, just east of Oak Island, Pe-shau-ba and the boys set several nets to test the fishing. The morning brought exciting results: walleyes, northerns, whitefish and even a huge muskie that had caught its many sharp teeth in the twine and hopelessly wrapped itself in the net.

"Yes," Pe-shau-ba concluded, speaking aloud but really talking to himself, "Even the fishing is good. When we return, this is where we shall settle." Then, remembering his young fishing companions, he turned to them and said, "What do you think? Shall we start a new village here?"

Both boys replied in the affirmative—with enthusiasm.

On the way back to camp the fishermen stopped on a rocky island and harvested seagull eggs for breakfast.

Later that day, several hours after breaking camp, the party stumbled across a small settlement of Ojibway at the Angle Inlet. Here they stopped to visit. Pe-shau-ba wanted to make certain there would be no objection to a new village in the area. When the locals were told there would be no more than eight or ten families at the most—they assured Pe-shau-ba the Ottawas would be most welcome. As their chief put it, "There are some advantages for us. We, too, are a small village and although the Sioux have not been seen on the lake for some time, it will be good to have friendly neighbors just in case."

Pe-shau-ba and the chief smoked the pipe of peace, exchanged gifts and assured each other there would be feasts of friendship when they returned the next spring.

As the small band proceeded south towards Rainy River, Johnny's mind was filled with exciting thoughts of the future, and he told his traveling companions more than once, "Of all the places I have seen, this is the lake I would most like to call home."

The trip up the Rainy River was pleasantly uneventful, and when the village on the lake itself was finally reached there was a joyous reunion with Win-et-ka, Maji-go-bo, and the children. Win-et-ka was very much pregnant and this gave the women much to talk about. Meanwhile,

Johnny filled Maji-go-bo's ears with tale after tale of the family's adventures the past two years since last they were together.

After resting a few days, Pe-shau-ba and his men, Waus-so, Sa-wing-wa, and Say-git-to, said their farewells and resumed their journey to Lake Huron—promising to return with their families the next summer when they would join Net-no-kwa and Johnny, and hopefully Masqua and Wa-me-gon-a-biew and their families, in developing the new village on the Lake of the Woods.

The prospects of such an adventure gave Johnny much to dream about in the months that followed.

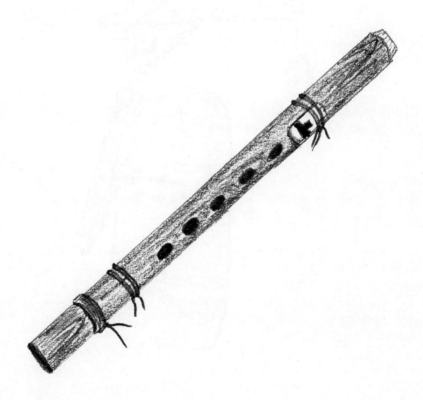

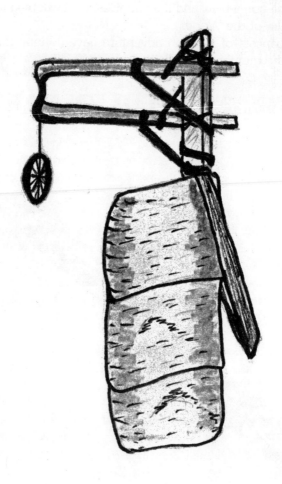

CHAPTER XIV
STOLEN EARTH

Once Net-no-kwa, Johnny and Ka-ka-ge-shig had constructed their lodge, the family settled down to the pleasant routine of summer living. As the time drew near for Win-net-ka to have her first child by Maji-go-bo, Net-no-kwa suggested to the boys, "Why don't we build a cradle board for the new baby?"

The idea did not meet with a lot of enthusiasm, but for lack of anything more exciting to do, the boys took on the project and over the next couple of days the cradle took form. A board about two feet in length was hewed out of pine for the back. A curved piece of wood was attached at the base as support for the child's feet. Birch bark was fitted as the front of the container and was bound to the back by thongs and bands. Net-no-kwa decorated these bands with beads and porcupine quills. A hoop of willow was fastened over the top of the board from which a light cloth could be hung to protect the child. Toys made of straw and birchbark were dangled from the hoop for the child's entertainment. When it was complete, moss was stuffed into the bottom. This would serve as a diaper and, of course, would be replaced from time to time. The cradle board was designed for carrying on Win-net-ka's back or for standing by itself. This would be home for the baby most of the first year.

The project was completed none too soon, as Win-et-ka gave birth to a son early one morning within that same week. She called him "Hole-in-the-day", because a patch of blue sky could be seen through the heavy overcast that cloudy morning.

It was the custom in the village for the male relatives of the father and mother to do mock battle for the possession of the newborn child. Maji-go-bo's relatives formed the defense and it was the obligation of Win-et-ka's family to steal the child. Since Johnny and Ka-ka-geshig were the only males on the mother's side their task was impossible but they were determined to conform to tradition and give it their best try. Maji-go-bo's relatives met the boys' good-natured attack with pails of water and then picked them up bodily and carried them to the lake where they were unceremoniously thrown in again and again, but in the process, everyone became soaking wet. Finally the youths were allow-ed to escape so they could capture the baby. They then marched around the fire singing a traditional song which included the words, "We have caught the little bird." In the end it was Maji-go-bo's obliga-tion to give gifts to the winners to ransom his new son. Had the sides been more evenly matched, the free-for-all would probably have been a bit more serious. As it was, there was plenty of commotion—and that was the whole idea—to make the child brave by hearing so much noise so soon after it was born.

As fall approached, Maji-go-bo shared a concern with the teenagers, "As you have probably heard me say, last winter was a most difficult one for our village. The beaver seem to have some kind of disease and have become very scarce. Other fur bearers haven't been very plentiful either. The only good thing is that there have been plenty of rabbits and caribou to feed our people. Anyway, some of us are thinking of setting up a trapping camp many days' journey from here to the southwest in an area where no one has trapped or hunted for a generation because it is a sort of "no man's land" between the Ojibway and the Sioux. We would leave our families here along with enough hunters to keep them in food."

Maji-go-bo paused just long enough for Johnny to interject, "Will you take me and Ka-ka-geshig with you? We have both seen 16 summers and can hunt and trap as well as any brave. We would be of great help to you."

Maji-go-bo smiled for effect, paused tantalizingly, and then said, "If I had not planned to take you with me, I would not have told you this soon."

"What will your mother say?" Ka-ka-geshig asked.

"I have already talked with her", Maji-go-bo said to their surprise. "It is all right with her."

During the next few weeks, the boys thought winter would never come, but eventually preparations were under way. The most time con-suming task was preparing hundreds of arrows, because rifles would be used only in an emergency for self defense should they encounter the Sioux. If guns were used in hunting, the noise would give the camp away in case there were enemy Indians in the area. Hundreds of hours were spent practicing with bows and arows until every brave felt he could shoot consistently with a high degree of accuracy. Johnny had never had to rely on the bow and he practiced nearly twice as long as most.

Shortly before the first fingers of ice appeared on Black Bay, more than a score of braves set forth down the Rainy River, then west along the south shore of Big Traverse to the cross-country route to the Red River which was then followed south to the Red Lake River, and when the Thief River joined that stream they turned their canoes north. The journey would have been only a fraction as far by land, but the longer distance by water was well worth it. When they arrived at what is now called Thief Lake, a site was selected on the south shore a short way from where the river left the lake, which could be easily defended from attack. The location chosen was a natural clearing where any hostile forces would have to expose themselves to the protected defenders. Before leaving their Rainy River village the leadership had agreed to copy the whiteman in the construction of a stockade around their lodges. No nails were used because of the noise the pounding would make. Instead, the cedar posts were lashed together with watape (spruce roots). A good supply of meat was laid in should there be an attack or siege.

When all was secure, trap lines were laid out and everyone went to work. There were no overnight camps away from the Fort for fear of the Sioux. Because no one had hunted or trapped in the area for many years, animal life was in great abundance. Johnny and Ka-ka-geshig teamed up with Maji-go-bo and there was a steady harvest of furs every day—beaver, martin, fisher, otter, mink, fox, lynx, and even a few wolverines. Everyone agreed they had never experienced such successful trapping.

Evenings were spent skinning the day's take and stretching the hides—normally women's work. One night as Maji-go-bo was skinning out a particularly difficult wolverine he observed, "This is just one more reason I miss my wives!"

Maji-go-bo also missed his dog team; they had been left behind for fear their howling and barking would give away the location of the camp.

There were so many moose and deer in the area that even hunting with bows and arrows was quite productive when necessary.

Best of all, the Sioux never made an appearance.

Late in the winter, just when everything seemed to be going so well, a three day blizzard hit the area. No one dared venture out of the lodges—let alone the fort. As the storm finally subsided, bitter cold set in and no one was anxious to resume work. When the temperatures finally began to moderate, the job of locating the traps and digging them out began. The new snow was powdery fine, and snowshoes were of little value—it was all work. The job had to be done, however, and one by one the traps were reclaimed, most of them empty. The deep snow meant the end of the movement of animal life and trapping became totally non-productive. The big game, such as moose and deer, simply yarded up and stayed put. Actually, no one was especially concerned about the trapping. Far more than a normal year's harvest was already within the stockade, but the food supply had become dangerously low. Even the meat stored for an emergency was about gone. Although there was little danger of actual starvation, the men were growing hungry and dissatisfied with their meager rations. It brought back memories for Johnny of the difficult winter at Sabaskong Bay on Lake of the Woods. Among those memories was the medicine hunt inspired by his mother's dreams that ended in the harvest of three moose and saved the village from starvation. As the situation grew more critical, Johnny reminded Maji-go-bo and Ka-ka-geshig of the incident and said he would like to try fasting and praying to see if the Great Spirit would give him a similar vision of where to find game. When Johnny said that he would have to go off by himself and be alone, Ka-ka-geshig was concerned, "What about the Sioux? You would be helpless by yourself!"

"I'm not too worried about that," Maji-go-bo interjected, "No one is moving in all this snow."

"Besides," Johnny assured him, "I won't go far—just a little way into the bush. If I am not back in three or four days you can check on me."

"Maji-go-bo told the others of Johnny's plan and no one objected. As one of the braves put it, "Right now—anything is worth a try."

Johnny left without delay—taking with him enough hides to make a shelter. Because poles could not be dug into the frozen ground or bent without snapping in the cold, he constructed a teepee, similar to those used by the plains Indians. The enclosure was made small so that a little fire would keep the room warm. Two layers of hides were used with air space in between for insulation. Johnny took no food with him and ate only snow for moisture. For three days he did nothing but fast and pray and sleep. Actually he prayed out loud and when there was no response, he prayed a little louder to be sure he had the attention of the Great Spirit. Again and again he would implore, "Oh, Great Spirit, who has given visions and dreams to my mother to save our people from starvation, hear my prayer! Show me where to find game—amen."

Although Johnny had long since forgotten his English tongue, he remembered that he had been taught to end his prayers with "amen". And so each time he prayed he concluded his loud Ottawa petition with a soft, single word of English.

On the night of the third day, as he was growing weary from the fasting and emotional outpouring, the teepee suddenly became as bright as day. A handsome young man with long yellow hair and skin fairer than his own seemed to materialize through the smoke hole and set foot in front of him. Johnny was speechless, but the angelic creature spoke these words, "What is this noise and crying I hear? Do I not know when you are hungry and in distress? I look down upon you and it is not necessary that you call upon me with such loud cries."

Suddenly there was a vision of a setting sun casting shadows on the snow, and the heavenly visitor went on, "Do you see those tracks?" Johnny managed to whisper, "Yes, they are the tracks of two moose."

"I give you those two moose to eat."

With that, the young man lifted the door flap and disappeared into the night, even before Johnny had the presence of mind to thank him. While the doorway was open, he saw that it was snowing and knew that any tracks he found in the morning would be fresh. Overwhelmed by the whole phenomenon, Johnny sat in deep thought for a time. "Had it been for real? Or was his mind playing tricks on him?" Finally, he curled himself around the coals of his fire and fell asleep.

In the morning he looked outside. The snow had stopped, so he picked up his bow and arrows and took off into the bush without thought of direction—literally plowing a trail as he went. There was absolutely no doubt in his mind that he would find tracks—and find them he did. He followed them as fast as the waist-deep snow would permit until he came over the very first rise of ground and there came upon a cow moose and her yearling calf, feeding on a fallen cedar. The animals were in easy range and Johnny dropped both of them with a single arrow each. It wasn't until he was "gutting them out" that the full significance of the moment sank in and only then did he begin to shake with excitement. Laying aside his knife, he paused to sing a song of thanksgiving to the Great Spirit.

Johnny returned to camp as quickly as he could—huffing and puffing from exertion and emotional exhilaration. Ka-ka-ge-shig was on guard duty as his cousin came floundering through the snow and he had the gate open before he was even close. Johnny was breathing so hard he could scarcely talk, but the words finally tumbled out—"Got two moose. . .had a vision. . .saw messenger from Great Spirit. . .came into my lodge. . .promised two moose. . .got two moose!"

The commotion aroused the entire camp and everyone came running. Johnny was an instant hero.

Long before the two moose had been consumed, the spring thaws began and further danger of starvation was at an end. By the time the ice began to leave the rivers and lakes the trappers had broken camp and were on their way north. The story of their heroic efforts soon became legend among the Ojibway and their allies, and the area where they had trapped came to be called "stolen earth". The English translation used the word "thief", and from this event then came the names "Thief Lake", "Thief River" and Thief River Falls"—all important places in the geography of Minnesota.

MINNESOTA

CHAPTER XV
STOLEN FURS

The return journey was planned via the Red River and Pembina, where there were both Northwest and Hudson's Bay trading posts in operation and where the men hoped to do some trading on their own rather than at the post by their village where they would have to endure the help and advice of their women folk. Unknown to them, however, the Chief Factor at the Northwest post was a scoundrel and tyrant named Wells who completely dominated the Indians of the area as they had become indebted to him. He was equally malicious in his treatment of the small group of halfbreeds he held in his employ. In order to keep everyone under his control he refused to give credit in the fall of the year against the winter harvest of furs—a custom that had been observed in these parts ever since the La Vérendryes had been on the Lake of the Woods.

When the Rainy Lake band of trappers arrived at Pembina, Wells made contact immediately and invited them to his post. His hospitality was disarming and before long they were partaking of his rum, apparently as his guests. Only Johnny and Ka-ka-geshig were left out—not because Wells had any concern about their age—but because Maji-go-bo made it clear there would not be any for them. Having seen so many times what liquor had done to his family and friends, Johnny would not have partaken anyway, but with the adventurous Ka-ka-geshig, it would probably have been a different story.

The trappers had endured a long and difficult but successful winter and they had worked hard. In their minds they had sufficient cause to celebrate—and celebrate they did. The thought never occurred to anyone that there may have been a sinister purpose behind the rum. In an hour or so the braves were dead drunk and scattered all over the trading post grounds. Johnny and Ka-ka-geshig, meanwhile, were lounging about the interior of the trading post, when a sudden flurry of acttivity sent them into total shock. Wells' halfbreeds entered the store carrying most of the bundles of furs they and their friends had worked so hard to accumulate during the winter! They walked right past Johnny and Ka-ka-geshig, ignoring them, and at Wells' direction, plac-ed the furs in his bedroom. Wells then closed the door and locked it.

Ka-ka-geshig was devastated. He leaned against the wall and slowly slid down into a sitting position on the floor—eyes and mouth wide open—speechless.

Johnny reacted just the opposite. Anger and indignation welled up within him as he straightened up to the full six feet he had attained over the winter. Shoulders back, chest out, he took six quick strides and blocked the path of Wells as he turned from the locked door. Wells was short and fat—very fat—from years of soft living at the expense of others. Although Johnny was only turning seventeen, he was every inch a man. His body had responded remarkably to the rigors of the wilderness and he was well muscled beyond his years. He stood a full head taller than Wells and his steel blue eyes stared hypnotically down into the squinty, pig eyes of the fat man.

Although he knew his adversary was only a boy in years, Wells sens-ed he could not handle him physically—or at least he did not want to take a chance on losing to someone so young. Having made that deci-sion, he quickly drew his handgun and pushed the barrel into Johnny's midsection. To Wells' surprise, it was like pushing against cast iron. Every muscle in the youth's body was like spring steel. The thought even flashed through the man's mind that his bullet could not penetrate anything that hard.

Up to this point, Johnny's actions had been totally reflex—without logic. All he could think of was the hard winter's work all for nothing and the gall of this trader who no doubt planned to tell the Indians when they sobered up that they had traded most of their furs for rum. As he stood there, nose to nose with the tyrant, the cold gun barrel against his stomach and a half dozen of Wells' halfbreeds in the room, he finally realized the seriousness of the situation and that he could very well be facing death, but he just didn't care. He was not going to back down. He did, however, finally begin to use his head. Choosing his words carefully, while still staring into his adversary's eyes, Johnny spoke, slowly. . .deliberately. . .coldly. "I am armed only with a knife; I will now take that from my belt and throw it away; that is how much concern I have for you and your gun!"

Slowly but steadily his hand moved to the knife, pulled it from its sheath, and flipped it into the wooden floor where it quivered for endless seconds.

"Now I am totally unarmed. Would you shoot me even so, *Squawman?*"

Wells made no move. Johnny grasped the wrist of the man's gun hand and slowly pushed it to one side and then began twisting it. The trader tried to resist but he was no match for the youth whose every muscle was toned by anger and hate from the thought of losing the best harvest of furs ever and of what Wells was doing to his people. The pain in the wrist was excruciating; the trader let out a cry and dropped the gun. As it hit the floor a shot rang out—but the ball fired harmlessly into the wall.

"You cry like a rabbit!" Johnny sneered as he retained control with his right hand and then, with his left, slapped both of the bully's fat cheeks as hard as he could, again and again.

"Help me!" Wells cried out, but there was no response.

Johnny encircled the man's flabby leg with his own and gave him a mighty shove that sent him sprawling on his back. He then addressed the bedroom door—which didn't look all that solid. He gave it a quick blow with his shoulder and the wood splintered around the lock and swung open. Johnny turned around and spotted Ka-ka-geshig still sitting in a trance on the floor and called out, "Come, my cousin, we have work to do!"

As the youths carried the first bundles past Wells, he reached out and grabbed at them, breaking the twine on one pack and spilling the furs on the floor. Johnny stooped over and calmly re-tied the bundle. Wells screamed in frustration, "Stop them! Stop them! They are only boys!"

The only answer came from one of the hired help as he walked out the door and shot back over his shoulder, "If they are only boys, you can stop them as well as we!"

At this point some of the Rainy Lake Indians entered the lodge—aroused by the shot. Maji-go-bo grasped the situation immediately and ordered his men to help carry out the furs. Only minutes later, all of the band and their harvest were safely over the river.

Wells finally realized the gravity of his situation. Not only had he lost a chance to procure a large quantity of fine furs, but he had totally lost control of the Indians in the area as well as the respect of his hired hands. Hoping to cut his losses, he sent an emissary across the river with a horse as a personal peace offering to Johnny, and he offered to pay a fair price for the furs. Johnny ignored the offer and the men took their business to the Hudson's Bay post instead.

Johnny's heroic action established him immediately as a leader of his people in spite of his youth. Word of his conquest of the hated Wells spread among the Indians over a wide area and from that time forth, Johnny was treated with respect by all who met him.

But in all the fuss, Ka-ka-geshig's adulation perhaps meant the most to Johnny. For here was a youth of his own age whom he had once feared and he had been genuinely surprised when he defeated him in their confrontation back at the Red River when they had first met. Now he stood nearly a full head taller than his cousin and no longer gave away a weight advantage. Ka-ka-geshig simply said—with awe and admiration in his voice—"And to think I once thought I could beat you up!"

For Johnny, that said it all. He had arrived. He had begun his Indian life as a village fool—knowing nothing of the ways of the wilderness and being pushed around by everyone. This day he had become a true brave in his cousin's eyes and in his own.

CHAPTER XVI
The FALCON

Upon the return of the trappers to Rainy Lake, Johnny was treated like a real celebrity. Old men called him by name, women whispered as he passed, young braves visited and joked with him. And the boys of the village just wouldn't leave him alone. Johnny loved every minute of it. Little did he realize that the experiences of the past few months had him well on the way to one day becoming a chief in his own right.

One afternoon, a week or so later, when Johnny had wandered up the lake shore to be alone and to dream about the future village on the Lake of the Woods, Wa-me-gon-a-biew and No-din-ens and Masqua and his family arrived from Red River. Ka-ka-geshig saw them come in and while helping them unload, poured out story after story about the adventures of the past winter. He was especially strong in his praise of Johnny and when he described his cousin's physical growth and maturation to Wa-me-gon-a-biew, he "laid it on pretty thick" and gave the impression the white boy had turned into a young giant.

"And where might I find our hero?" Wa-me-gon-a-biew asked.

Ka-ka-geshig didn't know but Net-no-kwa replied, "I think you will find your brother down by the lake—up the shore to the right."

Wa-me-gon-a-biew loped off in that direction. Ka-ka-geshig started to follow but his older cousin stopped him and said, "Please, Ka-ka-geshig, I would like to see him alone; there is much we must talk about as brothers."

The truth of the matter was that Wa-me-gon-a-biew knew Johnny wouldn't have forgotten the promise of a wrestling match when next they met, and from all he had heard about how much his brother and changed, he wasn't so sure he could still handle him and wasn't at all anxious to have any spectators around should he lose—least of all, Ka-ka-geshig.

He had not gone far out of the village when he spotted Johnny sitting alone by the lake with his back propped up against a big white pine. Without making a sound he stalked within 10 yards of him before saying in a threatening voice, "On your feet, white boy! Let us see if you can fight like the brave you think you are!"

Johnny, of course, knew his brother's voice immediately, and as much as he would have liked to give him a proper welcome, he didn't say a word but slowly got to his feet, just as slowly turned around, and then in a lightning move assumed the stance of a wrestler—feet apart, arms outstretched, hands in front and moving constantly. Wa-me-gon-a-biew responded in like manner and they circled each other like a couple of whitetail bucks about to do battle. Only the smiles on their faces belied any malicious intent. After more than a minute of these preliminary rituals, they came together with a crash, chest to chest, each trying to throw his brother to the ground. Johnny's new height proved to be a decided advantage as he finally bent his brother over backwards and dropped him with his own full weight on his chest. Quickly Johnny swung his body perpendicular to Wa-me-gon-a-biew and managed to lock his brother's arm between his legs in a scissors. It was then fairly easy to control the right arm with both of his. Wa-me-gon-a-biew bucked and twisted again and again but with his brother's full weight on him, he only succeeded in wearing himself out. Johnny knew victory was inevitable and savored every minute of it. Each time Wa-me-gon-a-biew made a move he ended up more helplessly in the grasp of the human vice that held him, and each time Johnny would ask, "Give up?" or "Had enough?"

Again and again the reply was the same, "Never!"

But finally, totally exhausted, Wa-me-gon-a-biew muttered, "You win."

Johnny, however, wasn't through with him. He pretended to let his brother up but then wound his long muscular legs around Wa-me-gon-a-biew's middle and dropped him once again on his back. The older brother was too exhausted to resist.

"Now, my brother," Johnny teased, "You and I have some things to talk about! Remember that time on Yellow Girl Point when you pushed my face in the sand and I got a mouth full of gravel? Well, this is for that!" And Johnny gave his legs a mighty squeeze.

Wa-me-gon-a-biew grunted.

"Oh my," Johnny observed. "Your belly has grown soft on No-din-en's cooking—you old married man! And how about that time you over-loaded the hand gun and it nearly knocked me out? Well, this is for that!" and he squeezed again.

Wa-me-gon-a-biew gasped as the air went out of him.

Johnny had dreamed of this day for years and had every intention of recalling every time his brother had gotten the better of him and then taking his revenge again and again, but at the thought of the old muzzle-loader whacking Johnny on the forehead, both brothers began laughing uncontrollably and the wrestling match was all over.

As they rolled apart and sat up, Wa-me-gon-a-biew said, "This might surprise you, but I am truly proud that I have so young a brother who is so good a fighter."

More than an hour of conversation followed as the young men shared their experiences of the past winter and spoke intimately of their thoughts and dreams as only brothers can. When Johnny told of how he and Pe-shau-ba and the others planned to build a new village on the Lake of the Woods, Wa-me-gon-a-biew responded, "There is nothing I would like better than to be a part of that plan."

"Good," Johnny said, "I had hoped you would say that."

As the boys got to their feet to return to the village, Johnny clamped a playful headlock on his brother and reminded him, "You have always said that when the day came when you could no longer handle me, you would no longer call me *"Little* Falcon." What, now then, shall be my name?"

Wa-me-gon-a-biew thought for a second and then responded, "That is easy—from now on you shall be known as *The* Falcon."

And so it was for the rest of his life, that John Tanner was known to everyone—white and Indian alike—as "The Falcon".

The dreams of the new village on Lake of the Woods came to pass. It was here that the White Indian eventually had a family of his own and when old Pe-shau-ba grew too old to govern he named The Falcon as his successor. From this base, he led his men on many an adventure. He also encouraged his people to grow crops (on Garden Island) and led them to a better way of life.

Even though The Falcon traveled far and wide over his long and exciting life span, and even though he was eventually reunited with his white family (and that's another story!) this most beautiful of all lakes remained his first love.

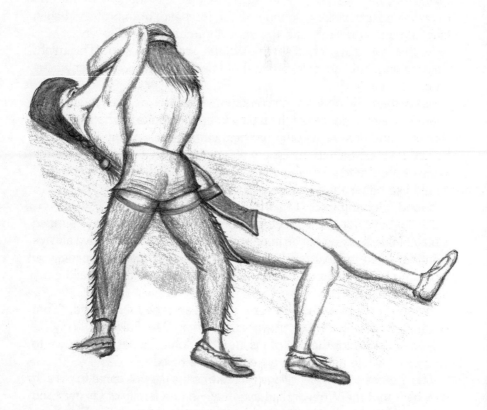

EPILOG

Yes, there was a John Tanner, but he was better known as "The Lake of the Woods Falcon". As chief of his own band he protected them from exploitation by the white traders, and, under his leadership, helped them develop a better way of life than most tribes of that time. He even developed a program of farming on Garden Island where his people raised such crops as corn, pumpkins, potatoes and squash.

Although The Falcon was recognized on the Lake of the Woods for his leadership of his people, he is better remembered for his adventures away from the lake. When Lord Selkirk, a chief partner in the Hudson's Bay Company, needed help in his private war with the Northwest Company, it was The Falcon who guided his mercenary Swiss soldiers and furnished some of his own braves in a successful drive to recapture a string of forts. He, personally, led a night attack over the stockade surrounding Fort Douglas and won the victory without firing a shot.

Lord Selkirk was so grateful to The Falcon that he awarded him a small pension for life. When he heard Tanner's personal history, he offered to provide funds for a search for his family. At first The Falcon protested. He may have said, "It would be no use, old Manitou-geshig said he killed them all and brought me my brother's hat as proof."

But Selkirk probably countered with, "How do you know the hat wasn't stolen and shown you just so you wouldn't try to escape?"

Tanner admitted that possibility existed and the search was commissioned. It is difficult to imagine the emotions the man must have experienced when he was told his father had died of natural causes, but that all other members of the family were still living!

When The Falcon traveled to Ohio for the reunion, he wore Indian clothing and could scarcely remember a word of English. He actually met his brother, Edward, on horseback traveling in the opposite direction to a neighboring community. He knew who he was because he looked exactly like his father as he last remembered him—but he was in such a state of shock he could not speak!

The family, of course, treated John like someone who had returned from the dead. They did their best to convince him to stay and return to the life of a white man, and he did make an honest effort—for about a year—but was really not happy and in the end chose to return to the Lake of the Woods. Over the years, however, the family did remain in touch and they occasionally saw each other.

And what of The Falcon's own family? He took two wives, as permitted by the customs of his people, and they bore him several children, but only a son and two daughters grew to adulthood.

With one of the wives (Red Dawn) the marriage was apparently something less than happy. When The Falcon was on one of his journeys he left that wife and the two daughters at the Rainy Lake village. While there, she became involved in a romantic affair with one of the braves and later when John picked up his family on his return, his rival (who was unknown to him) lay in ambush, shot him, and left him for dead. Fortunately, he was found by a party of Hudson's Bay officials who brought him to the trading post on Rainy Lake. The chief factor at that time was Dr. McLoughlin,[1] probably the only physician within several hundred miles. Under his professional care, The Falcon was nursed back to full health.

We do not know what happened to the treacherous brave. The marriage was reborn but did not work out. However Tanner retained custody of the girls for a time and eventually enrolled them in school at Sault Ste. Marie. Tanner's son chose to remain an Indian, but in later years became a missionary.

After 1830, The Falcon spent considerable time at Sault Ste. Marie where he met Dr. Edwin James, an army surgeon. We owe this man a great deal, for it was he who wrote down for us the life story of John Tanner up to that point. The doctor and The Falcon also collaborated in the translation of the New Testament of the Bible into Ojibway. It was published in 1833.

Tanner met and knew well many of the great explorers of his day: Major Stephen Long, General William Clark (of Lewis and Clark), Major Delafield, John Riply and Governor Cass of the Michigan Territory.

---

[1]McLoughlin was actually away when Tanner was brought in, but returned to care for him. McLoughlin later transferred to the west coast and became known as "The Father of Oregon."

The Falcon's last adventure away from the Lake of the woods was in the employ of the United States Government as a guide to the famous explorer, Henry Schoolcraft and other officials. At that time, Schoolcraft was the regional Indian agent and stationed at Sault Ste. Marie. For some reason, Tanner did not get along with Schoolcraft's brother and when the man was murdered, The Falcon was accused of committing the crime. Actually, he was not guilty and the real culprit eventually confessed (a U.S. Army officer named Tilden). Meanwhile, loving freedom and not having a great deal of confidence in white man's courts—John fled. Sometime later a skeleton was found in a nearby swamp and at first it was assumed to be that of Tanner. This would have been a tragic end for so heroic a figure. Fortunately, there were many reports of The Falcon being seen thereafter on the Lake of the Woods, and we would surely like to believe they were true. A man such as this deserved to live out his days among his own people on the lake he loved best.

John Tanner.